How could she have kissed him back?

And it hadn't been any demure, friendly kiss, either. Even so she still reeled from wanting more. Wanting him. She'd thrown all of herself into that moment. All her pent-up longings and unfulfilled dreams. All her unfocused energy now had a focus—*passion.*

Passion and Sam Armstrong. She halted and groaned aloud. Great going, she scolded herself. In one evening, she'd undone all the progress she'd made this last year.

Tonight she'd slipped, but it wouldn't happen again. They were neighbors, and that was all they could ever be.

Dear Reader,

Happy Valentine's Day! We couldn't send you flowers or chocolate hearts, but here are six wonderful new stories that capture all the magic of falling in love.

Clay Rutledge is the *Father in the Middle* in this emotional story from Phyllis Halldorson. This FABULOUS FATHER needed a new nanny for his little girl. But when he hired pretty Tamara Houston, he didn't know his adopted daughter was the child she'd once given up.

Arlene James continues her heartwarming series, THIS SIDE OF HEAVEN, with *The Rogue Who Came to Stay*. When rodeo champ Griff Shaw came home to find Joan Burton and her daughter living in his house, he couldn't turn them out. But did Joan dare share a roof with this rugged rogue?

There's mischief and romance when two sisters trade places and find love in Carolyn Zane's duet SISTER SWITCH. Meet the first half of this dazzling duo this month in *Unwilling Wife*.

In Patricia Thayer's latest book, Lafe Colter has his heart set on Michelle Royer—the one woman who wants nothing to do with him! Will *The Cowboy's Courtship* end in marriage?

Rounding out the month, Geeta Kingsley brings us *Daddy's Little Girl* and Megan McAllister finds a *Family in the Making* when she moves next door to handsome Sam Armstrong and his adorable kids in a new book by Dani Criss.

Look for more great books in the coming months from favorite authors like Diana Palmer, Elizabeth August, Suzanne Carey and many more.

Happy Reading!

Anne Canadeo
Senior Editor
Silhouette Books

Please address questions and book requests to:
Silhouette Reader Service
U.S.: 3010 Walden Ave., P.O. Box 1325, Buffalo, NY 14269
Canadian: P.O. Box 609, Fort Erie, Ont. L2A 5X3

FAMILY IN
THE MAKING

Dani Criss

Silhouette

ROMANCE™

Published by Silhouette Books

America's Publisher of Contemporary Romance

For Dan, my first and only love,
on our twenty-fourth wedding anniversary
and all the others yet to come

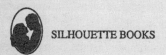 SILHOUETTE BOOKS

ISBN 0-373-19065-4

FAMILY IN THE MAKING

Books by Dani Criss

Silhouette Romance

Family in the Making #1065

Silhouette Intimate Moments

Sheriff's Lady #490

DANI CRISS

has wanted to write romance since she first read Jane Austen's *Pride and Prejudice*. In high school she dabbled in poetry and short stories, though in her mind, the words "short" and "story" are a contradiction in terms.

She squeezes her writing time between work as an office manager and taking care of her family. She lives in Kansas City with Dan, her wonderful husband of twenty-four years, her two lovely daughters, Crissie and Sara and a varying assortment of pets.

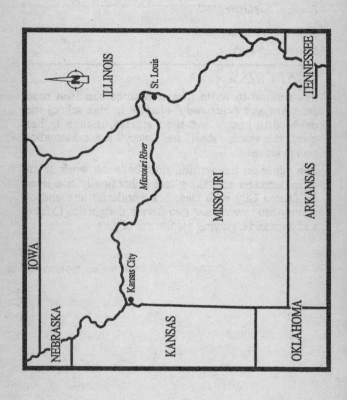

Chapter One

Sweat gleamed on his sun-browned body. A body that epitomized masculinity. A body that any female, from high school to retirement age, would stop dead in her tracks and drool over. His chest was broad, his abdomen taut, his arms and thighs solid muscle that flexed with his easy running. The golden highlights of his light brown hair shimmered in the spring morning sun.

From the driveway of her new home, Megan McAllister watched this perfect male specimen make his way up the street. His sleeveless T-shirt sculpted his torso in a way that set her senses on full awareness.

Joan Jacobs, the realtor standing beside her, sighed. "What a hunk. He's the most eligible bachelor in town." She winked at Megan. "And that's where he lives."

Joan pointed to the house on the west edge of the lawn. She was moving in next door to him, Megan realized with a tremor of trepidation.

"I'll introduce you," Joan continued as his long, powerful strides carried him toward the foot of Megan's driveway. "Hey, Sam."

Megan waited as his smooth gait slowed. He recognized Joan and waved a salute, peered at the loaded Honda and at Megan, then stopped. He pulled the hand towel from the waistband of his scandalously skimpy gym shorts, wiping his brow and neck as he came closer.

When he stopped in front of Megan and Joan, he grinned, showing two deep dimples and laugh lines around the darkest, liveliest sapphire eyes Megan had ever seen. Engaging, electric and devastating. A killer smile. And he'd just aimed it at her.

"This is Megan McAllister," Joan said as Megan fought her unwilling response to the wattage in his dimpled grin.

"Sam Armstrong." He extended a hand to Megan without taking his unwavering gaze off her, even when he inclined his head in the car's direction. "Looks like you could use some help moving in."

"I'd settle for having my hand back."

She pointedly eyed her hand still lost in his firm grip. His grin widened and his mesmerizing eyes flashed with amusement. Her heartbeat stuttered. The man was TNT to her senses.

"Joan, you didn't mention my new neighbor has a terrific sense of humor," he said, reluctantly releasing Megan's hand.

Nor had Joan mentioned that Ms. Megan McAllister was very attractive. Individually her features were not that dramatic, but together they added up to an understated beauty. Her long dark brown hair accented the gentle lines of her cheekbones, her pert nose and her wide eyes. Soft brown. Soulful. They captured his attention and drew him in.

She was on the thin side, but her body was softly curved in all the right places. The top of her head reached the top of his shoulder—the perfect height for his six-foot frame.

And the lilt in her voice. He liked it very much. "You have an accent," he said. "East Coast? North of the Mason-Dixon line."

She nodded. "Boston."

"What's brought you to the Midwest?"

"A new job." Megan found herself wanting to tell him more, all the reasons she'd had to leave her home and friends so far behind, why she'd had to start over. There was something about him that made her think he would be so easy to talk to.

But she couldn't, her heart warned in alarm. She couldn't let him—let anyone—get that close again. Things had changed. New city, new house, new firm to work for, and a new me, she'd vowed from the moment she'd begun packing. The woman she'd become in the last nine months was very different from the trusting, carefree woman she'd been.

"I'd better get the house opened up," she said. "The moving truck should be here shortly. It was nice to meet you, Mr. Armstrong."

"Sam," he said.

"All right. Sam. Thanks for the offer of help."

She smiled at him, allowing herself to soften, to relax her guard a little. But only a little, her mind cautioned. She had to keep her distance, though she sensed that with this man, it would be very hard to do. Keys in hand, she strode to the front door, unlocked it and went inside, leaving him standing in the spring morning sunshine.

"Interesting," Sam murmured, watching Megan's slender figure as she walked past the picture window in the living room, then past the dining room bay window. "So, Joannie, tell me what you know about her."

"Besides what she told you? She's single and a C.P.A."

"That's all you know?"

"That's it." She shrugged.

"Come on," he persisted. "You're the best realtor in all of Kansas City and you're even better at extracting a person's life history without their realizing they're giving it."

"This lady was very reticent. Sorry, but you'll have to find out what you want to know on your own."

She sauntered over to her car, leaving Sam to ponder the best course to take. He wanted to know more about his new neighbor. Her reticence piqued his interest, that and her figure. He shouldn't be allowing his thoughts to stray in that direction, but he couldn't stop them. Deciding he'd start by being helpful, he reached into the car's trunk and hefted the first box.

Standing at the kitchen sink, Megan gazed out the window at the well-kept lawns that bordered hers. This was a well-to-do area of south Kansas City. Most of the homes had been built in the seventies.

Her first glimpse of the area had given the impression of peacefulness and stability. According to the realtor, Megan, at twenty-eight, was the youngest homeowner in the neighborhood. Sam Armstrong must be the second youngest. He couldn't be more than three or four years older, she mused, then quickly tore her thoughts away from him and to her neighbor to the rear.

The man was planting a tilled section of his yard for a garden. Home-grown vegetables—maybe she would try her hand at it, not throw herself so totally into her work this time. Maybe this time, in this place, she could regain the balance, find the little pleasures in life Fate had stolen.

But what would she do about Sam Armstrong? The way her heart had hammered at the sight of his smile was a clear indication she could fall for him. Just like she had for

Randy, the captain of the high school football team, and Marc, the sweet-talking stockbroker with a heart of stone.

Then there'd been Alex. Of all the wrong choices she'd made concerning men, he was the worst. She wrapped her arms around her abdomen, the pain still fresh in her mind.

"This one's marked art supplies," a male voice said from the doorway.

She turned to see Sam Armstrong carrying a box from her car. She'd left the trunk open and he'd taken that as an invitation.

"Where do you want me to put it?" he asked, shifting the weight in his arms, calling Megan's attention to where it had no business being—his muscled biceps.

She pointed to the countertop. "Thank you," she said once he'd set down the box. She didn't want to send him away, but she knew she had to.

"Do you paint?" he asked before she could say what needed to be said.

"Yes. Watercolors mostly," she found herself saying. "Some sketches."

"Ever sell anything?"

She shook her head. How could she tell him how personal her drawings were to her? They were her solace, her relaxation, her pleasure.

"Ever tried?" he persisted.

She had to chuckle to herself at his enthusiasm. "No, but I have framed a few pieces over the years."

He nodded as if that met his approval. She was surprised at the surge of warmth that gave her. Warning bells rang in her head.

"I'll grab another box." With that he turned toward the doorway.

"No, Sam. Thanks, but I can manage the rest," she told him, hoping she didn't sound as agitated as she felt. "I'm sure you have plans."

"None that won't keep for the few minutes it'll take us to unload your car."

Us? Accepting his offer of help wasn't wise, caution warned, especially when his gaze traveled over her figure. There was a languid heat in his eyes that called to the woman in her, urged her to surrender to her undeniably strong longings. Now more than ever, Megan couldn't afford to let down her guard.

"It's kind of you to offer," she began, "but I—"

"Can manage. So you said. But do you really want to turn down willing-and-able shoulders?"

Broad shoulders. Strong. Megan wanted to lean on them, on him. When he smiled that disarming, very sexy smile, her resistance threatened to fade like a hazy memory. She could use a shoulder to lean on just a tiny bit, but time and again she'd learned the only person she could count on was herself.

"The movers will be here shortly," she insisted. "They'll help me unload the car."

Sam studied her for a long moment. The lady was polite about it, but he sensed her wariness. Perhaps he was being too pushy.

"Well, I'm just next door," he told her. "If you have any problems, I hope you'll feel free to call."

She nodded and smiled slightly. Sam wondered at the trace of regret he saw there for that brief moment. Or had he imagined it? It had come and gone across her delicate features so quickly.

Filing the impression away, he turned and headed back through the house the way he'd come in. Megan followed a couple of paces behind. They reached the front door just as the moving van pulled up to the curb. Two burly men got out of the passenger side, waiting in the grass while the driver maneuvered the truck into the driveway.

"With all that help you should be settled in no time," Sam said amicably.

"Thank you," she said, wondering if he realized she was expressing more than just her gratitude for his help. Amazingly he seemed to understand her need to maintain a distance between them. Instead of crowding her, he was giving her room. She would never be able to tell him how much she appreciated that, she thought as he stepped off the small porch and started toward his own home.

"Uncle Sam! Uncle Sam! It's a *big* truck!"

Megan blinked at the sound of the young voice. A golden-haired child darted across her lawn and into Sam Armstrong's embrace. He laughed as he scooped her up. Megan felt her heart constrict. The child and the man. So happy together...

"Where?" he teased. "I don't see any truck."

The little girl giggled. "Turn around, silly. It's right there." She pointed to the moving van backing up the drive, then aimed her stubby index finger at Megan. "Who's she?"

"Our new neighbor." He set the child back on her feet and took her hand in his. "Come and meet her."

Our new neighbor. Megan replayed the words in her mind as the pair strolled toward her. Did his niece live with him?

"Becca," he said to the girl, "this is Miss McAllister."

The little girl craned her neck to get a good look at Megan. Megan sat down on the porch step so they were eye level.

Becca slid her hands into the pockets of her worn jeans and gave Megan's face a solemn once-over. "Hello, Miss Muh... Muck..."

"McAllister," Megan supplied the name. "But you can call me Megan."

"Uncle Sam says I shouldn't..." She looked up at her uncle.

He ruffled a gentle hand through the girl's curls. Megan noted the tender gesture and felt her heart's resolve give a little.

"It's okay this time," he said, "since Megan's last name is hard for you to say, and since she said you could."

She gave Megan a shy smile that revealed dimples not quite as deep as Sam's. Her elfin features were brightened by crisp blue eyes that shone with intelligence and curiosity. Megan longed to touch the cap of curls on Becca's head, to feel the beautiful baby-fine strands caressing her fingers.

"I'm five. And I go to kindergarten," the girl said.

"That's exciting for you, isn't it?" Megan felt tears of loss threaten. She'd moved halfway across the country, hoping to escape memories triggered by familiar sights and sounds. But, like her best dishes, they'd been packed for travel. A brief conversation with a little girl and the hurt was unwrapped, dusted off and just like new.

"You Ms. McAllister?" a gruff-voiced man asked.

"Yes." Megan got slowly to her feet and nodded to the man with the clipboard. "You should be able to get everything in through the garage. I'll go in and open the doors for you."

"And that's our cue to leave," Sam said to Becca as the man started back to the truck.

As the two walked away, Megan heard Becca ask what was in the truck and heard part of Sam's patient reply. For the next hour she directed the moving crew, but her thoughts returned often to Sam and his niece, how the girl came to be living with him, how comfortable with each other the two

appeared to be, how he hadn't been the least bit conde-
scending when he spoke to the girl.

Several times Megan had to wrench her thoughts from
Sam to which box went in which room and where to place
the few pieces of furniture she'd brought with her. But each
time her mind wandered back to Sam and Becca. The rap-
port between them. The laughter they shared. The affection.

Would she ever be able to see a child and not remember?
Not feel the ghosts crowd in?

Freshly showered, Sam stepped out of the bathroom to be
greeted by the aroma of vanilla extract. In the six months
since he'd inherited responsibility for his orphaned niece and
her baby brother, he'd come to know that scent meant
cookies. Gooey, soft-centered chocolate chip, if he was
lucky.

With the kids' arrival, Sam's life had changed dramati-
cally. They were all still adjusting, but some of the changes
were definitely for the better, he had to admit, toweling his
hair as he followed his nose to the kitchen.

Becca and his housekeeper, Emmaline, spooned dough
onto a cookie sheet while ten-month-old Brian banged two
wooden spoons on the metal tray of his high chair. When he
spotted Sam in the doorway, the boy let out a squeal and
double-timed his tuneless rhythm.

Sam chucked him under his drool-coated chin. "Oh, boy.
Heavy Metal. And before lunch, yet."

Brian giggled. Of the three of them, the baby had handled the transition best. Although, he had to admit Becca
had made tremendous progress lately.

"We're baking cookies for Megan," she announced.

Sam stood behind her, noting the way she stuck out her
tongue as she concentrated. Chuckling, he dipped a finger

into the glass mixing bowl, scooped out a dollop of dough and popped it into his mouth.

"Dr. Armstrong," Emmaline scolded good-naturedly. "I've trained your niece to use a spoon."

"Now you have to teach Uncle Sam." Becca laughed. "Can we take the cookies over to Megan right when they finish cooking?"

"If that suits your uncle's schedule," Emmaline said as she carried the cookie sheet over to the oven.

"Can we?" Becca asked him.

"Why not? I don't have much of a schedule today." Besides, he would grab at any excuse to see her again.

"We all need time off to play. That's what you keep telling me, right?" Emmaline closed the oven door and straightened. "And don't worry, Dr. Armstrong. I doubled the recipe so there'll be plenty left for you and the kids."

He put an arm around the older woman's ample shoulders. "Emmaline, you're a treasure."

"Go on with you," the housekeeper said, blushing. "First batch will be ready in fifteen minutes. Time enough for you to comb your hair."

"And me," Becca added. "I want you to fix my hair, too, please."

Sam's eyebrow quirked at his niece's statement. A momentous occasion when she asked him to do her hair. He wasn't very good at it. Most of the time the tangles wouldn't come out and the bows usually wouldn't stay in. Today, though, to look her best for a visit with Megan McAllister, she was willing to endure his inexpert ministrations. She even did so with a minimum of squirming and complaints, too.

A half hour later they walked outside, plate of cookies in hand, to discover the moving van and Megan's car were gone. No one answered their knock at her door.

"Where did she go?" Becca asked.

"I don't know." But it had taken them less than an hour to move her in. The lady traveled light, it appeared.

"Is she coming back?" There was a trace of fear in Becca's little voice.

Sam bent down until they were eye-to-eye. "Yes. She will be back," he assured her with a long hug. "Maybe she just went to the store."

Becca's lower lip pouted but her eyes did brighten at the knowledge that Megan wasn't gone from her life forever. "I hope she didn't buy cookies."

"Well, even if she did, they won't be as good as ours."

"That's right!" Becca asserted with an emphatic nod of her head. "Emmaline and me make the bestest cookies."

Sam was so glad to see her cheerful again that he didn't even correct her grammar. "Right. Let's go grab some lunch and see if we can't talk Emmaline out of some cookies for dessert. We'll come back later and see if Megan's home."

"Okay, but I want to have my lunch on the porch."

So she could watch for Megan's arrival, Sam knew. Interesting, he mused. A few minutes in her presence and Becca was totally captivated.

Of course, he admitted he, too, found the woman more than a little intriguing. She looked lithe and sexy, her legs long, her dark hair caressing her face, her skin creamy and soft. He still remembered the feel of her hand in his.

And her eyes. There was something about them—a haunted look. Most of his patients had that same look when they first came to him for help in dealing with the conflicts and pain in their lives.

He didn't think he was mistaken about the emotions he'd read in Megan's expressive eyes. As he helped Emmaline get Becca situated on the porch, he wondered if Megan had come to Kansas City hoping for a new start. Sometimes that was the first step in healing, leaving the place and persons involved behind.

The idea that someone might have hurt her made him downright angry. Unusual, he mused as he busied himself with paperwork after lunch. As a psychiatrist, he was accustomed to maintaining an objective distance. Odd to find he couldn't do that with a woman he'd only spoken to for a few minutes.

He put down his pen to puzzle through his feelings. There was attraction. That had been immediate and strong, though out of character for him. Knowing how tough relationships could be, he was generally slow to get into one, preferring to really get to know the other person first.

With his new neighbor, though, he liked what he saw and he definitely wanted to get to know Megan McAllister. But totally out of character for him was the fierce longing to protect her. He wanted to hold her, to heal her hurts. And not the way a psychiatrist does with a patient, but rather the way a lover does. That knowledge had him doing a mental double take. His feelings were moving way too fast for his comfort.

The slam of the front screen door broke through his thoughts. Then came the soft patter of five-year-old feet racing down the carpeted hallway to his den.

"She's back! Megan's back!" Breathless, Becca burst through the doorway, crayon in one hand and a paper in the other. "I'll get the cookies."

"Whoa," Sam said, stopping her rush out of the room. "What have you got in your hand?"

"A picture for Megan." She proudly held up the drawing.

For Megan. To Sam's surprise, it hurt the tiniest bit to have her share her creations. Not that he didn't have plenty of them tacked up on his den walls—fifteen at last count, and there were more in a drawer. Early ones, mostly. Ones too painful and personal for her to display. They'd been a form of therapy, a way to get the child to deal with her grief and fears. What she couldn't express in words, she could sometimes get out on paper.

There was happiness and sunshine in this latest work of hers, but he knew Becca was still very fragile. He hoped Megan, an artist herself, would see the beauty in a two-dimensional drawing of a barely recognizable house, four stick people and a three-legged dog.

"Come on," he told his niece. "Let's go get those cookies."

The girl tore down the hallway and rounded the corner into the kitchen, nearly colliding into Emmaline's stout body. The housekeeper merely laughed and handed Sam the plate heaped with cookies.

Becca raced through the living room and was out the front door in a flash. Sam followed at a more sedate pace, sidestepping the crayons scattered on the porch, and praying this trip to Megan's wouldn't turn out to be a bad idea. Becca was so excited. And while Megan had been good with his niece, he wasn't sure she wanted their company. He took a deep breath as Becca stretched to ring the doorbell.

A lot more than the child's welfare rode on how Megan accepted their overtures, he realized. He didn't want her to turn them away, and his reasons were purely personal. He wanted to get to know her. Just that suddenly. He breathed deeply to steady his rattled peace of mind.

As Megan tucked the sheet around the corner of the mattress, she heard the doorbell. She straightened, trying to convince herself that it could be another neighbor who'd seen her moving in and had come to welcome her. But as she peered through the small window set in the front door, she saw Sam standing there.

Her palms were clammy and she swiped them across her jeans before opening the door. Sam looked incredibly sexy in fitted khaki slacks and a yellow knit golf shirt, his brown hair neatly combed. She had to squelch her runaway hormones and that incomprehensible longing to lean into his solid, gentle strength. The urge made the words that would send him away lodge in her throat.

"We brought cookies!" a little voice said excitedly.

Megan looked down and realized Becca stood next to her uncle—a sprite with a hopeful grin on her cherubic face. There were freckles scattered across her nose and cheeks.

"Cookies?" Megan echoed inanely.

"Uh-huh. And I made you a picture." She held up the paper in her hand.

While Megan stared down at the drawing, Sam watched the parade of emotions cross her lovely face. Pleasure changed to pain and pain gave way to panic. His earlier impression was right. She'd been hurt. Badly. He wanted to comfort her. Mixed with that was the need to protect his young niece. He could see Megan was having a hard time dealing with the feelings the crayon drawing evoked, but he doubted he could make Becca understand if Megan refused the picture.

"Honey, maybe Megan doesn't have a place to hang it."

Through the rush of emotion that assailed her, Megan heard the words Sam said, words to protect a child's fragile feelings. She looked down and saw Becca's small face start to crumple.

"I have the perfect place for such a pretty picture," she found herself saying. She couldn't hurt the child, no matter what the price would be to her own heart.

Though she'd had no intention of inviting Sam into her home, she found herself doing just that. For Becca, she told herself firmly as she led the way to the kitchen. They placed the picture on the refrigerator and anchored it with two butterfly magnets she'd unpacked only moments ago.

"Thank you, Becca," she said. "It's just what the kitchen needed."

As he set the plate of cookies on the butcher-block countertop, Sam looked around, noting there was no table, no chairs. There'd been only one rocker in the way of living-room furniture. On it sat an oversized stuffed gray-and-white floppy-eared rabbit.

"Did you go to the store?" Becca asked.

Megan frowned at the question. "No. Why do you ask?"

"We came by before lunch and you weren't here," Sam explained. "I told her you might be at the store."

Megan made a face. "I was at a pay phone trying to find out why my electricity hasn't been turned on today. They say they lost the work order."

"Then you're without power." A plan was taking shape in Sam's mind. "For how long?"

"Until sometime Tuesday. They don't work on the weekend and they've already booked up Monday."

"Then I think you should have dinner with us."

"Yeah!" Becca shouted gleefully.

Megan's breath caught. She couldn't accept his offer. She was much too aware of him, of the way he seemed to fill the kitchen with his masculine presence. Aware of her own weakness.

"No," she told Becca gently. "I couldn't impose."

The girl's brow furrowed. "What's that?"

"It's nonsense," Sam inserted, looking at Megan. "You can't cook and you can't even keep milk to go with the cookies because the fridge isn't on."

"Yeah," Becca intoned. "You have to have milk to duck your cookies in."

"She means dunk," Sam corrected at Megan's puzzled expression. "Have dinner with us tonight."

Becca radiated her eagerness for Megan to accept. Megan knew she was losing control of this situation. Who was she kidding? She'd lost control the moment Becca had held up that sketch. She should stand her ground, but when she gazed into those crisp blue five-year-old eyes, she faltered.

"All right." The words were out before she could catch them and she couldn't take them back. She only hoped she wasn't heading straight for disaster.

Chapter Two

As Megan walked toward Sam's house, she mentally lectured herself on keeping her best interest in mind. She was an easy mark for his charm and sex appeal. His virility drew her, more than any other man's had. Much more.

The understanding he'd shown her was partly responsible, she supposed, and his thoughtfulness in bringing cookies and inviting her to dinner. Alone in a new city, she was especially vulnerable to the gesture. She'd moved here, hoping to find a happiness to fill the void in her life, and she'd made a start at it already. She wouldn't do anything to jeopardize that.

After he'd left her house, she'd tried to come up with a plausible reason to back out of the dinner engagement, but the truth of the matter was she wanted company. She'd spent too much time alone lately.

It was neighborly of him to ask her to dinner, and Becca would be there, so it wasn't a date. If he even started to suggest a date for another night, she would stop him, explain that she wasn't ready for another relationship.

Becca spotted her as she started up the wooden porch steps. "Megan's here," she shouted as she pushed open the screen door.

Megan had to smile at the girl's enthusiasm, but now that she was here, her steps hesitated. This close to being in Sam's house, to seeing him again, she realized the company she'd most wanted was his. But before she could follow her instinct to run, Becca took her hand and pulled her into the house.

The living room was spacious, masculine in its earth-tone decor, but here and there a child's additions stood out—a small chair and table littered with books, an overflowing toy box in one corner, a blond, pigtailed Cabbage Patch doll on the recliner.

Sam walked in, wiping his hands on a kitchen towel. Light brown hair covered his tanned forearms. The knit yellow shirt stretched tantalizingly over his well-defined torso. His smile, full of warmth and welcome, showed those two alluring dimples of his. The picture of masculinity and power nearly took her breath away. No man had ever looked so sexy to her.

Megan knew she should run for the door, but Becca's firm grip on her fingers kept her rooted to the spot. Under the spell of Sam's smile, she felt her willpower explode into a million fragments and scatter like ashes in the wind.

"Uncle Sam is cooking dinner." Becca giggled. "He's making a mess in the kitchen and it's a good thing Emmaline isn't here to see it."

Sam scowled at her with mock menace. "You weren't supposed to tell."

Becca giggled again, and Megan had to laugh. "Who's Emmaline?"

"My housekeeper." Sam supplied the answer. "She's off tonight."

"And you're on duty." Megan smiled at the thought of Sam puttering around a kitchen, putting together dinner for her and his niece. What would it be like to come home to that scene every night? To a warm and caring welcome? Would that ever happen for her? she wondered.

Then a miniature whirlwind charged in on hands and knees and latched onto Sam's ankle. A baby boy. His round little face was smudged here and there with chocolate. His brown hair, a bit long and baby-fine, curled on the ends. His big blue eyes watched Megan with interest while he babbled merrily.

Everything in the room faded into the background. Becca was saying something, but Megan couldn't make out the words over the rushing in her ears. Her memory launched her back to the past, to days that had been almost unbearable. It had taken all she'd had just to get through those days and nights, to keep from giving up. She'd lost so much. She'd tried to put the past behind her, but she hadn't succeeded as well as she'd thought.

Becca paused in her introduction of Brian and looked up at Megan. Sam realized Megan hadn't heard a word his niece said. She stared at Brian, her face white, her eyes filled with pain. The awareness and attraction he'd seen when she'd first come in were replaced by shock and anguish. All she was going through was there in her face. In her lovely eyes.

"Megan," he said, walking toward her.

She didn't answer. She appeared ready to bolt out the door. Sam couldn't let her do that, but how could he stop her? She was hurting, and he'd never felt more helpless.

"Becca, take Brian to his room and see if you can interest him in some toys, okay?"

Becca must have sensed Sam was concerned. Without a protest, she got down on her hands and knees and coaxed her brother down the hall to the bedroom.

"Megan, what is it?" Sam stood in front of her, waiting for her to see him. Her gaze was unfocused, as if she were lost in some terrible memory. "Megan," he repeated more sharply.

The rough sound of Sam's voice penetrated the memories. Blinking, Megan realized she'd blanked out at the sight of the little boy. All she could think about was Joey. Her son. The baby she'd never even gotten to hold. So beautiful. Tiny and fragile. His life had been so short.

She read concern in Sam's expression, but she couldn't tell him about her horrible loss. And she couldn't stay for dinner. Not now. She wouldn't be able to handle the reminders. She tossed a strangled apology over her shoulder as she rushed out the door.

Sam swore under his breath. He couldn't let her go, not when it was clear that she was hurting. He had to do something, but what? He didn't have a clue where to start.

With Brian a few steps behind her, Becca walked into the living room. As the screen door slammed behind Megan, she looked from it to Sam, her expression puzzled and hurt.

"Where's Megan going?" she asked.

"Home. She, uh, doesn't feel well." Sam drove his hand through his hair, thinking. He scooped up the baby and carried him to the family room, placing him in the playpen. "Do you think you could watch Brian—really close—while I make sure she'll be all right?"

Becca nodded. "I'll play with him so he doesn't cry."

"Perfect. Thank you."

Sam gave her a quick kiss, then hurried after Megan. He caught up with her at the front door. Tears ran down her face as she fumbled to get a key into the lock. He caught her hand.

"Please, Sam. Just let me be—"

"No. I need to know what's going on." She hadn't asked for his help, wasn't his responsibility, but he had to know what had sent her running away from him.

He took the key from her trembling fingers, opened the door and ushered her into the living room. The evening shadows filtered through the picture window, chasing away the brightness. One last faint ray of sun found the lone rocker and the stuffed rabbit slumped on the wide seat. What secrets did that bundle of gray fur know?

Sam glanced from it to Megan. She stood in the center of the room, her arms wrapped around her abdomen, tears glistening on her cheeks. He longed to hold her close, but the stiffness of her shoulders warned him that wouldn't be wise.

"Tell me about it," he said softly.

Megan shook her head and sniffed. She couldn't see his eyes clearly, but she heard the caring in his voice. She needed that caring. Had needed someone to care during all the long and painful days and nights when she'd been haunted by what she'd lost and all she would never have. It would be so easy to give in. And so unwise. Hadn't she learned that the one who gave love could also take it away? To tell Sam about the past would be to let him a little bit closer, to leave herself open to hurt.

"Becca needs to understand why you ran out. She likes you. A lot," Sam said sharply. "This is going to hurt her very much."

"I'm sorry—"

"Sorry isn't enough." He sighed heavily. When he spoke again, his tone had softened. "Megan, six months ago she lost her mother and father in a car accident."

Megan gasped. Becca knew loss as well as she did, and at such a young age. To have lost both her parents... The realization of what the little girl must have suffered ripped through her. And she'd only added to Becca's pain.

She should never have accepted the dinner invitation, but she hadn't been able to refuse. She'd wanted to be with Sam and his engaging niece. As a result, she'd hurt a beautiful little girl who'd been hurt so much already.

"The boy?" Megan asked.

"Becca's brother. Why did seeing him upset you so?" Sam asked, though he feared he already knew. He sensed her struggling with the answer and damned the lack of light in the room. He wanted to be able to see her face, her eyes. "Did you lose a child?" he prodded gently when she didn't answer him.

Megan nodded. Leave it at that, part of her silently begged him. That's all I can tell you. But when he pressed a handkerchief into her hand, the tears flowed and some of the words spilled out.

"He would have been close to Brian's age, if he'd lived. He was born ten weeks too soon." Much too soon. He would never laugh, never cry anymore. She would never hold him to her breast, never nuzzle his little face, never rock him to sleep or walk the floors with him at night.

"Oh, Megan..." The words were so inadequate, but there was nothing else Sam could say. His feelings for what she'd gone through swelled in his throat, in his heart.

"Joey was so tiny." Her voice cracked. "His lungs weren't developed enough. They tried everything. There were tubes everywhere in his little body."

Sam took a tentative step toward her, then a second and a third. Even more than before, he needed to hold her close. He didn't have the time or the inclination to analyze his reasons or think through the consequences of his actions. This once he went with his feelings.

Somehow Megan found herself in Sam's arms. It felt so good to be held, to lay her head on his very strong shoulder. He was warmth and badly needed comfort. The scent of him, even through her tears, made her want to burrow closer.

She felt safe, sheltered, cared for. She wanted to stay here forever, even while she knew that was impossible. All good things must come to an end, as Alex had mercilessly taught her.

"Megan." Sam sighed as her sobs abated. "I wish I'd known."

"What could you have changed?"

She felt him shrug. "I don't know. I guess I would have prepared you, at least."

Could anything have prepared her? She realized she'd avoided facing another infant or toddler since losing Joey. Older kids had been difficult enough to see and to deal with, but seeing Brian, a baby the same age as Joey would have been, had hit her much harder than she'd expected.

"I'm sorry, Sam, but I can't have dinner with you."

Sam understood. Still, he couldn't just walk away and leave her hurting. Couldn't walk away, period. She felt too good in his arms—fragile, vulnerable, and yet strong enough to endure. Her slight curves melded against his solidness so perfectly. He didn't know where this attraction was leading him, but he was going willingly.

"Tomorrow we can talk—" he began.

"No." Megan straightened and stepped away from him. Physical distance, if not emotional. He was asking for more than she could give him. Much more. There were so many reasons—ones she still couldn't tell him about.

Sam worried at the finality in her refusal. "You need to talk to someone," he said cautiously, not wanting her to balk. "I realize you might not be completely comfortable with me, but I can give you the names of a couple of colleagues—"

"Colleagues?"

"I'm a psychiatrist." He paused, gauging her reaction to his occupation. She frowned. A bad sign? He wasn't sure. "I just thought that if you wanted someone to talk to... Well, since you're new in Kansas City you might not know of anyone to go to. I needed someone for Becca. And for myself."

"Yourself?"

He nodded. "Becca's mother was my sister. She was five years younger, so I did a lot of looking out for her when we were growing up. And her husband was a close friend of mine."

"Losing them both at once must have been a terrible blow," she said quietly.

"Yeah." He breathed deeply. "Fate can be cruel. How can you make sense of it snuffing out the lives of two decent, loving people?"

"Or innocent babies."

"Yes. A loss like that... No one should have to go through that, but... Well, if you'd like, I can give you the names of a couple of friends who could help you work through things."

She shook her head.

"At least say you'll think about it." If that's all she could give him now, he would take it and try to be satisfied, try not to worry about her. But he'd misplaced his objectivity somewhere between meeting her and holding her while she cried, and he had a feeling he wouldn't find it anytime soon.

She affected him on a sensual and emotional level, drawing him in.

Megan's first impulse was to refuse, as she had refused the doctors back in Boston. She hadn't been able to talk about the horrible twist of fate that made her son be born too soon. Joey's death and all that had come after—his funeral, the divorce, the operation—she'd wanted only to be alone. But she'd come here to heal.

"All right. I'll think about it." She sighed. She wanted Sam to stay there, wanted to be in the warmth of his embrace again, but she had to send him away. No matter how very difficult that was. "You should be getting back to your family." *Family.* She would never have one of her own. No one would ever know how devastating that was to her.

"You're probably right," he said reluctantly. "Becca will be concerned."

"What will you tell her about my leaving?" she asked.

"The truth. She'll understand."

Megan nodded. The man was being wonderful about this. Generous and understanding, she thought as she let him out the door and closed it softly behind him. He was almost too good to be true. And something too good to be true was definitely too good to last.

She leaned her back against the door and realized she still held Sam's handkerchief. An omen that things between them weren't over.

She would see him again. How would she handle that? How could she put her attraction to him aside? After being in his arms and crying on his very willing and comforting shoulder, trying to deny that attraction would be harder than before.

Pressing his handkerchief to her damp cheek, she thought about how wonderfully consoling it had been to be held. For that moment, at least, he'd salved the hurt, assuaged some of the grief, made her feel less alone and empty.

Through all that, though, she'd sensed his resolve to not let her go. But there was no such thing as happily ever after. She'd buried that illusion with a tiny baby boy.

The memory of being in Sam's arms stayed with her as she sat in the rocking chair, hugging the gray rabbit to her chest. She watched out the window as one by one the neighborhood's ornate streetlights came on. In each of them was a promise that life was renewed each day.

Late the next afternoon Megan returned home after shopping for a few necessities—a battery lantern, an ice chest, a few nonperishable groceries to get her through until the electricity was connected on Tuesday, and a set of cushions for the window seat in the dining room. That was her favorite place in the house.

As she pulled into the driveway, she spotted Becca walking slowly across her lawn, a box in her hand. Megan eased her foot on the brake pedal and breathed deeply. She'd known this moment was bound to come, but still she wasn't ready to face the girl. What could she say to Becca? Sam was right. Sometimes "sorry" just wasn't enough.

She pulled the car into the garage, then took a second deep breath as she went out to meet the child. Becca eyed her earnestly, and Megan decided she would feel much better seeing the girl carefree and laughing again.

"Becca," she began, "I'm very sorry about last night."

"It's okay. Uncle Sam 'splained it to me." She held out a stationery box and waited for Megan to take it from her. "It's papers and crayons."

Megan grinned inwardly to know she hadn't dampened the girl's spirits completely. That meant a lot to her. If truth be known, since Sam had told her about Becca's parents,

Megan had felt a certain bond with her—a connection she hadn't felt with anyone for the past few months.

"Did you make another picture for my refrigerator?" she asked Becca.

"It's for you to make a picture."

"Me?"

Becca nodded, her blond curls bouncing with the movement of her head. "When my mommy and daddy died, I was scared and really sad. Uncle Sam taught me how to draw pictures about it."

"Draw about it?" Megan's breath caught. How could she begin to sketch the death of her fragile infant son and what had followed?

Becca nodded again. "Uncle Sam says if you draw about the scary and sad things, sometimes you feel better. It kinda helped me, I guess."

Megan marveled at the wonderful relationship Becca must have with her uncle. He'd had his own grief to deal with as well as his niece's. And the addition of two children into his bachelor life-style couldn't have been easy. Somehow he'd handled it, though. Excellently.

If only she'd had someone, Megan thought. Her parents hadn't understood what she was going through. Her world had come crashing down around her ears, but they'd expected her to pick herself up and go on as if nothing in her life had changed.

"Anyway," Becca continued, "I thought if you didn't have paper and crayons, you could use mine. I have lots."

Megan stared down at her. Nothing anyone had done had ever touched her as deeply as this gesture of caring—a little girl dealing with her own loss, reaching out to her, offering help and comfort. Others had tried, but Megan had firmly shut them out. Even her parents. How had Becca gotten through the barriers?

Megan tried to put her gratitude into words, but couldn't get them out around the lump in her throat. Then Sam's voice carried from the back door of his house, calling for Becca. Brian's crying could be heard in the background.

The girl shrugged matter-of-factly. "I gotta go. Sunday is Emmaline's day off, and Brian is being a crybaby. Uncle Sam says he's teething." She rolled her eyes. "Bye."

Becca darted off, leaving Megan alone in her yard, holding the box of paper and crayons.

What was she going to do about the girl? Becca was reaching out to her and wouldn't be denied. Megan didn't want to hurt her, but seeing the child meant seeing Sam, talking to him, having him close enough to touch, to hold.

She just couldn't handle that. It would be so easy to give herself up to the kind of caring he'd shown her yesterday. And so wonderful. But it wouldn't last. It never did, she'd learned. Not for her.

What would happen to her when their relationship was over? she wondered as she carried her purchases into the house. She couldn't take the risk. When she'd left Boston, she'd decided she didn't need another romance.

She'd wanted out of the apartment singles life-style, wanted to minimize her chances of repeating past mistakes. That had been top on her list of priorities. But she should have realized that in buying a house she would at some point come face-to-face with children in the neighborhood, see them play outside, hear their voices as they called out to friends.

While she put the groceries away, she contemplated looking for another house. She could rent this one out for the monthly payments plus a little extra. It would be a solid investment.

But she couldn't keep running forever. As she fitted the slate blue and mauve print cushions on the window seat, she knew this place was home. Sitting there, she gazed out at the houses and oak shade trees and carefully tended, fertile lawns. There was peace here. She'd felt it the first moment Joan had shown her the house and had driven her around the neighborhood.

She'd run halfway across the country. Now it was time to stop. Time to make a future for herself. Starting with the garden. Yes, she thought, feeling the burden on her shoulders lighten a little. She would plant seeds and watch them grow. Not just vegetables. Flowers. The house needed flowers. A planter box or two on the back deck. Roses, too, maybe out front or along the back fence.

Here she could find some sort of contentment. Even living next door to the most desirable man on the continent, his small family, and all the pain and feelings of emptiness that watching the children grow would bring.

In the bedroom closet Megan located a box and pulled out a roughly bound bunch of papers—watercolor drawings and simple rhymes. A children's picture book about cats and dogs and colors. There were several more, but this was her favorite. She'd made it for her child, for Joey. He would never see it, never sit on her lap and point at the pictures.

She'd had such dreams, but none of them would come true. It was time to let go of her grief and create a new life for herself. She would turn her creativity in that direction, do watercolors of flowers for the dining room, make a garden every horticulturist would envy.

She found a pretty pink gift bag with a bit of tissue paper inside, tucked the book into it and penned a note: "To Becca, From Megan."

Bag in hand, she hesitantly made her way to Sam's yard and up the porch steps. Brian still cried, nothing serious, just a fussy, whiny cry. Megan couldn't risk seeing the baby again, or Becca, or Sam. Especially Sam. All night she'd wished for the comfort of his arms around her, his voice softly soothing her to sleep. Dangerous longings that she couldn't give in to.

She heard Sam's deep, rich voice croon to the baby, pictured him holding Brian. Sam would look so incredibly sexy. The sight of him, the gentle sound of his voice—she would be lost.

She hooked the bag on the mailbox and returned to her house and her new beginning.

Chapter Three

With a weary sigh Sam splashed whiskey into a glass, added ice and some club soda, then carried the drink into the living room. Slouched on the sofa with his stocking feet on the coffee table, he surveyed the debris around him.

Brian's toys lay scattered through every room in the house. Sam had emptied the toy box in here and the one in the boy's bedroom, desperate to find something, anything, to get the poor kid's mind off his aching gums for a while. And give Sam's ears a break from the crying. But nothing had stopped Brian's fussing for long.

On the TV, the anchorman and woman discussed the day's beautiful weather Sam hadn't had a chance to notice. He hadn't had a chance to clean up the kitchen. Hadn't even had a chance to glance at the newspaper. He'd hoped he could put Brian in his playpen in the backyard with Becca for at least thirty minutes so he could cut the grass in the front yard, but that hadn't happened, either. Nor had he managed to get Brian down for his afternoon nap. Even that much would have been a blessed relief.

The kids were in bed now. He'd checked on them awhile ago and, thank heaven, both were sound asleep. Becca with her favorite blanket pulled up to her chin and Brian with his pudgy little thumb in his mouth. But there was no guarantee that situation would last the night. Becca still had an occasional bad dream and Brian... Well, Brian was teething.

On days like this he missed Nancy and Jeff more than usual. Nancy especially. They'd been about as close as siblings could get. He missed that emotional connection with someone, and the deep friendship he'd shared with her husband. And, as much as he loved his niece and nephew, he missed the quiet evenings whenever he needed peace and solitude to regroup.

Six months ago he'd had no idea parenting could be so physically and at times emotionally draining. Doing it singly... Well, he had a new respect for those people raising children alone. The job definitely had perks, but even with Emmaline's housekeeping help, it wasn't easy.

With something between another sigh and a groan of exhaustion, Sam raised his glass in salute to the cluttered room. "To an unbelievably long 'one of those days.'"

He took a healthy swallow of the drink and eyed the room's devastation. How did Emmaline do it? There might be toys out, but the days she was in charge, the place had never looked like the aftermath of a bomb blast.

Maybe she had a cleaning lady come in after he left for the office, he decided, taking another drink from the tall glass. He certainly paid her enough she could afford it, and she was worth every penny. She was so good with the kids—knowing exactly when to spoil them and when to be firm.

She made it look so easy, he thought, finishing his drink. He dragged his tired body up, turned off the TV and lights, then quietly made his way down the hall to Becca's room. She was a restless sleeper, always getting twisted in the covers or throwing them off altogether. Tonight she was sprawled over the twin bed, lying on top of most of the blanket and sheet. As he gently adjusted the covers over her small form, the hall light shone on a book lost in the tangle with her.

The book Megan had given her, he realized, picking it up. The little scamp must have taken it to bed with her and hidden it under the covers. Very curious about the surprise gift, he tucked it under his arm, whispered a "Sweet dreams, darling," to Becca and closed the door. He contemplated looking in on Brian, but decided it best not to risk waking the boy. He couldn't face another round of the crying right now.

In his own bedroom, Sam stripped down to his briefs and crawled into the bed, not bothering to carry his jeans and shirt to the laundry hamper. He would take care of that in the morning. Right now he wanted to examine this treasure of Becca's.

The binding was a homemade affair, stiff green construction paper over cardboard, he guessed. The delicate pictures on the inside pages were lovely in their lively simplicity. Furry puppy dogs and fluffy, frisky kittens in shades of whites, grays, browns and blacks. The orange tabby with the blond cocker was especially riveting. Surrounding the animals was an assortment of trees, grass and bright flowers decorating each page. Watercolors, some muted, some vivid. All wonderfully done, capturing the beauty of nature and the charm of the frolicking animal babies.

Megan had done all this herself, he realized, glancing back at the title page. He turned to the rhymes and read each one twice to savor them and the watercolor drawings. The rhymes were singsongy and silly, but delightfully so. Perfect to engage a child's mind and set the imagination soaring.

The Megan McAllister who'd done this book—who made characters and colors come almost alive—was very different from the woman who'd moved in next door to him, Sam mused. Loss changed a person. The shattered pieces never fit together in the same way.

He hoped she could find the part of herself that rejoiced in the ridiculous and in all that was beautiful in the world. He wanted her to find the light and laughter and love that had been stolen from her.

He wanted to be the one to help her.

Wait a minute, Armstrong, he cautioned himself. A healthy dose of realism was needed here. He couldn't take on any more responsibilities. Between dealing with his caseload, his own emotional baggage over the deaths of two people he loved and adjusting to sudden single parenthood, his plate was overloaded now.

His first priority had to be the kids. They'd lost so much. And his patients... He'd cut back on his practice to be with Becca and Brian. Soon, before his partners rebelled, he'd have to go back to pulling his weight. That would leave him even less time.

It wouldn't be fair to Megan to ask her to let him into her life conditionally when he knew how little he had to give her in return. He couldn't let her come to rely on him when there was every chance in the world he might not be able to deliver.

The thought made him frown, but his gaze found the book Megan had made and he smiled. Tomorrow—before Brian got up, he hoped—he would snuggle with Becca in her bed and read her Megan's book. Maybe he would have time to read it twice before he left for the office. He loved starting the day with the sound of her infectious little-girl laughter.

One day he wanted to hear Megan laugh, see more than that sad smile that didn't quite reach her eyes. An all-out, no-holding-back joyous laugh. One day... On that thought, he set the book on his nightstand and turned off the lights.

Thursday evening. Megan's first two days working for the accounting firm of Carstairs, Bains and Kelly had gone very well, but she was looking forward to the weekend. Monday she'd gone to the branch library and checked out several books on vegetable gardening and one very thick tome on roses.

She'd read them all, studying the sections on the vegetables that were easiest to grow. Since she was doing this for the very first time, she wanted to start simply. So, she'd decided on green onions, tomatoes, peppers, green beans and peas. She'd figured the northeast corner of her yard would be the best spot. It got the morning and early afternoon sun and shade during the worst of the day's heat.

Picking up her rough sketch of the garden, she went outside to pace off the space she would need to till this weekend. Her backyard neighbor was in his garden, carefully checking over his tiny seedlings and small plants. He would have a wealth of information, no doubt. She walked over and introduced herself.

"Ah, the pretty accountant," Mr. Jack Henderson said, shaking her hand across the chain-link fence.

"How did you know...?"

"Sam told me." He inclined his gray head toward Sam's yard. "A doctor, you know. *And* a very handsome young man." Mr. Henderson waggled his bushy eyebrows suggestively.

Megan sighed inwardly. All week she'd fought to repress the memory of being in Sam's arms. It hadn't worked. This evening she'd noticed him in the yard when she'd first come outside, noticed how incredible he looked in jeans and a short-sleeved polo shirt, playing with the children. She wanted to hear the sound of his voice again, to see his sapphire eyes gaze down at her with blatant interest, to experience more of his tender understanding. The lure to go to him was remarkably strong.

Dousing her attraction to him would be harder than she'd figured. At the moment he was absorbed in throwing a ball to Becca and rolling it to Brian.

"Don't you love the sound of children laughing?" Mr. Henderson asked.

Megan nodded, her eyes on the young boy. His giggles carried to where she stood, filling her with an incongruous mixture of heartache and a desire to laugh. She smiled. Maybe things would get better for her.

"So, what's the paper in your hand?" Jack Henderson asked.

She showed him the diagram of her proposed garden. He was putting in the same vegetables as Megan as well as garlic, lettuce, broccoli, carrots and radishes.

"Do you think what I've got planned will keep me in produce?" she asked.

He chuckled. "You'll be swimming in it. If we don't get too much rain, or it isn't too dry this summer. Here, you never know about the weather. It's the middle of April and the temperature is in the sixties, but we could still get a late freeze."

"Then should I wait—"

"No," he insisted. "If it cools down that much, you come out and cover them. I'll show you how. But first you have to get the ground tilled. Let's get Sam over here."

Sam. Megan's heart fluttered in panic. She wasn't ready to see him again. She still felt too vulnerable from the evening she'd cried on his shoulder, but before she could stop him, Jack called out to Sam, asking him to come over. He scooped up Brian and settled him on his shoulders as he and Becca trooped through the fence gate separating their yards and over to where Megan stood.

Her heart stumbled at the sight of him with the children. He could have been their father, such was the affection between them. Then her breath caught when he smiled his dimpled smile and gazed over her with a barely concealed warmth that heated her from the inside out. The breeze lightly ruffled the ends of his hair, making her long to feel the rich strands run through her fingers.

"Hi, Jack," he said. "Megan." His voice glided over her like a caress. One she shouldn't long for, but did.

"Hi." She smiled back, hoping her greeting hadn't sounded as breathless as the memories made her feel— memories of his warm, secure embrace, of the delicious sensations being near him had given her, of his caring.

"Megan made me a book," Becca announced to Mr. Henderson.

"She did?" The older man's eyes widened, sharing in Becca's excitement. Megan could feel his caring was very genuine. But then, who could look into the girl's lovely face and not be drawn in?

"Yes. It's the bestest book you ever saw!" Becca turned to Megan and to her surprise, hugged her around the middle. "Thank you."

Megan had to swallow past the lump in her throat. That her simple creation had touched the little girl... The pleasure was indescribable. "You're welcome. I'm glad you enjoyed it."

"I enjoyed it, too," Sam added. "It's warm and tender and funny."

With any other man, she might have thought the words were empty flattery, but there was something in his eyes that told her he had genuinely appreciated her creative efforts. It gave Megan a wonderfully warm glow.

Brian, still perched on Sam's shoulders, got bored with watching the adults and pounded on Sam's head.

"Hey, you rascal." Sam swung him down and set him on his hands and knees. Brian let out a squeal of laughter and took off for the deck. "Becca, can you keep an eye on him for a moment?"

"Okay." She charged after her brother, who giggled and crawled away as fast as he could.

Chuckling, Jack shook his head. "Such energy. So how's the teething going?" he asked Sam.

Sam rolled his eyes. "Most days we have a few good moments and a few more bad ones. When his gums do bother him, nothing seems to help for long."

"Then I'll take them both on Saturday, if you're free to till a plot for Megan's garden."

"No," Megan fairly gasped, then realized both men were staring at her curiously. But she couldn't have Sam any more involved in her life. She was much too susceptible to his charm. "That is ... I can manage—"

"Not Jack's ancient machine, you can't." Sam folded his arms across his wide chest, his stance proclaiming his determination.

Again Megan had to tamp down her desire to give in. She couldn't risk getting to know him, though that's exactly what she wanted. "I'll buy a shovel...."

Sam heard the alarm in her voice, saw it in her eyes. She was afraid to be around him. Did it have to do with Brian's reminding her of the past, or was it more personal? But if that was the case, then why did she practically devour him with her eyes every time she looked at him? Though he reminded himself he wasn't looking for a relationship right now, the puzzle that was Megan intrigued him more each time he was around her, and he couldn't seem to stop it.

"Shoveling won't be good enough," Jack told her. "The ground's never been turned for a garden."

"And I have experience using Jack's tiller," Sam stated.

Jack rubbed his shoulder. "Bursitis. Since the machine is too heavy for me to handle now, Sam gets my garden started at the first of April and tills everything under after the weather gets too cool."

"How about nine-thirty, Saturday morning?" Sam asked Jack, bypassing Megan altogether. He should be taking the lifeline she was throwing him. Then why was he so damned determined to spend some time with her?

"Fine by me. I'd better get inside. I'm waiting for a call from my grandkids." He waved and turned toward the house.

Megan watched while Jack walked away. Indignation burned in her eyes, turning the brown to the color of dark chocolate. Sam decided to ignore that gleam of defiance. He didn't want to do battle with her. There was a vulnerability about her, a certain something in the depths of her eyes, the firsthand knowledge that life wasn't always fair and didn't always follow a person's wishes.

But there was more to his interest in her, and it was pure male lust for the lovely package of femininity that was Megan McAllister. The strength of that shocked through him.

Megan raised her chin a defiant notch. The situation had gotten away from her in the blink of an old man's eye. She didn't know what to say, but somehow she had to get her plans for her garden back on track. A track that didn't include one very virile man who already occupied her thoughts far too much.

The blue of his eyes was mesmerizing. That deep rich sapphire—if she were to paint them, which she wasn't even considering, she'd have a difficult time conveying the intensity of color captured in those eyes. And the dimples—he was smiling at her now and it showed them off to full resolve-weakening advantage. How could such a boyish grin make him look so irresistibly male?

And how, after all that had happened to her, could she be so vitally attracted to another man, to Sam? While her logical mind had finally learned its lesson, her heart wasn't so smart.

"Sam, I—"

Her words were cut off by a high-pitched wail from the deck. Her heart lurched. Brian! He'd fallen on the wood steps. She stood paralyzed as Sam raced to the boy in several long strides. He lifted Brian into his arms, pulled out a handkerchief and tried to wipe at the boy's lower lip.

Blood. Megan's stomach clenched. Somehow she found herself standing on the deck steps next to Sam. Brian howled and squirmed, his head turning this way and that, his short, thick arms flailing at Sam's every attempt to examine the wound. All Megan could see was a drool- and blood-covered chin.

"I'm sorry," Becca said in a small voice.

Sam glanced at her intently while still trying to hold onto the toddler. "Becca, honey, it's not your fault."

"But I was 'sposed to watch him." The girl's lower lip quivered.

Sam tried to free an arm to draw Becca close to him. Brian let out a piercing shriek and twisted his small body. He didn't want to be held, and Becca needed to be comforted. He set Brian on the deck. Still crying loudly, the boy crawled over to Megan, grasping her leg and reaching a hand up to her. Sam froze.

Brian wanted *her* to hold him. Megan thought her heart would break, but she couldn't refuse his tearful plea. She sat on the top step, and he scrambled onto her lap. Her breath caught at the onslaught of emotions that hit her square in the chest—sadness and a sense of loss, then a feeling of wonder as he settled into her arms as naturally as if he belonged there. It had all happened in a heartbeat, but everything about this moment was forever scored in her memory.

"Megan...I...don't know what's gotten into Brian, to go to someone he doesn't know. Come here, Brian." He held out a hand, but the boy batted it away.

Sam knelt beside her, his expression a mixture of shock, apprehension and concern. Again he reached for Brian, but the boy only dug in deeper into Megan's arms. Even while it hurt to have him there where her own son should have been, it felt so wonderful. His sobs became small whimpers.

"It's all right, Sam." She inhaled deeply and let the breath out slowly, then offered him a tremulous smile. "This is what it would have been like to hold Joey," she mused quietly aloud. "I've always wondered..."

Sam eyed her intently. Her soulful gaze brimmed with unshed tears. She hurt, and there wasn't a damned thing he could do about it. Except be there beside her.

He sat next to her on the step, close enough his thigh brushed hers. She didn't pull away, he noted with pleased surprise. Sam handed her his handkerchief and watched as Brian let her dab at his injured lip.

Sam tugged Becca onto his lap and hugged her tightly. "See, honey, Brian's all right." He kissed the top of her head. "He's clumsy, and you can't help that."

"You're a wonderful big sister," Megan said, catching Becca's worried gaze. "And Brian only got a little bump. His tooth cut his lip a tiny bit, that's all."

"He bleeded on your shirt," Becca said pointedly.

Megan glanced at the red smear on her white T-shirt, then at the little boy in her arms. He'd dried his chin across the *B-O* on *B-O-S-T-O-N*.

"Small price to pay." She touched her fingertip to Brian's button nose, smiling back when he grinned up at her.

Sam wondered if Megan had any idea how alluring she looked at the moment, the child cradled against her breasts, her expression full of tenderness. She had to be thinking of her loss, but there was no pain in her eyes. Would that come later, when she was alone? He sincerely hoped not, but he sensed Megan didn't share her feelings easily. Except perhaps with children.

Becca yawned and her brother followed suit. Sam noted that the sun was low on the horizon and would soon be out of sight.

"I know two children who should be getting ready for bed," he said, tweaking Becca's nose.

"Brian's sleepy, but I'm not," she proclaimed around another yawn.

"Yeah, right." Sam glanced at Brian. "Hop up so I can carry your brother," he told Becca. But when he reached for the boy, Brian still refused to budge from Megan's arms.

Megan silenced his whimpered protest with a soft, "Shh, little one." He settled back against her, rubbing his face against her shirt once more. "Why don't I carry him?"

"Are you sure?"

She breathed deeply, knowing she was again leading with her heart instead of her head. Knowing how that had always gotten her into trouble in the past. She should refuse, hand Brian over to his uncle and let Sam handle him and the crying that would follow. But she might never experience the soul-swelling joy of another moment like this. The battle with her good sense was waged and over in a nanosecond.

"I have to quit running from the past sometime," she said slowly. "I guess there's no time like the present to start."

She wiggled the boy around until his head lay on her shoulder, then stood. He was heavier than she'd expected, but it was a welcome burden.

"Got him?" Sam asked.

Megan nodded and followed Becca to the gate. Sam walked beside her. Brian draped one arm around her neck and popped his other thumb into his mouth. The warmth of this moment would have to last her a lifetime.

Brian's small bedroom was decorated in bright colors with racecars-and-airplanes wallpaper along one wall. There was a shelf full of stuffed animals and books for the very young child.

Megan's steps hesitated in the doorway. This was the first time since the end of her pregnancy and the hysterectomy that she'd stepped into a little boy's bedroom. She'd planned to use dinosaur paper in Joey's, had even bought a stuffed dino that roared when squeezed and a brightly colored mobile to hook onto the end of his crib. She'd left it all behind.

"If you put him in the bed," Sam said quietly from behind her, "I'll get his clothes off. Hopefully without too much protest."

Megan garnered her resolution and crept up to the crib. The sheet was splayed with brightly colored cartoon characters. Sam lowered the side rail, and she gently laid the boy in the bed. He started to fuss, but as Sam crooned to him, he popped his thumb back into his mouth.

Overwhelmed by the touching scene and all the thoughts of how her life should have been, Megan turned to the doorway. Becca stood there, dressed in a pink nightgown, Megan's book in her hand. Megan recalled the girl's praise—''The bestest book.''

She glanced at Sam, softly speaking to his nephew as he changed him out of his play clothes, then to Becca. All she ever wanted—a little family of her own. But that would never be. So she would treasure the moment Becca cuddled next to her as she read the silly poems she'd written so many lifetimes ago.

Too soon the children were tucked in bed and she was alone in the living room with Sam, only to find that triggered a whole different host of emotions that were sensual and sexual and strong. She was setting herself up for trouble.

''Well, I should be going,'' she said.

Sam saw her look to the door and knew she was ready to bolt. Though it would be wiser to let her leave, he didn't want to.

''How about a drink?'' he asked.

Her eyebrow rose in surprise. Something flickered in her eyes, a longing to stay, he sensed; then the wariness was back. He should let her leave, but her being here, helping him put the kids to bed, made him realize how lonely he'd been.

''Please.'' He leveled his gaze at her. ''I could use some adult company.''

Her eyebrow raised another notch, but he saw the hint of a grin tug at the corner of her luscious mouth. ''You sound like a housebound mother who hasn't had a word with anyone over five years old in a week.''

''That's the way it feels. Oh, I talk to adults, but only patients or colleagues, it seems, and it's usually about business. I need away-from-the-office companionship.'' He caught the glimmer of interest in her eyes. "So how about it? One drink?"

Megan's resolve melted under the warmth of his hopeful smile. One drink. What could a few more minutes with him hurt? She had to admit she understood exactly how he felt. She needed some away-from-work company herself.

"Okay," she said, nodding.

"Great." His dimples deepened. "We have green Kool-Aid, apple juice, diet caffeine-free cola, milk. Or would you care for something stronger?"

"Diet cola will be fine." Megan didn't dare go for anything alcoholic. Not with her awareness of him so strong and her willpower weakening more by the moment.

She'd made the right choice, she decided as he returned from the kitchen with two glasses of cola. His cream-colored polo shirt stretched across his chest, defining the plane of solid muscle the fabric hid. The short sleeves banded around his powerful biceps. His jeans molded his lean hips and firm thighs. And when she recalled him with the two children, holding them, laughing with them... Virility and tenderness. All in all, he was a sinfully tempting package.

He handed her one glass and led her over to the couch, sitting close enough she could feel his body heat. With it came the desire to lean into it.

"Becca told me Emmaline doesn't stay to put the kids to bed," she said to redirect her wayward thoughts.

"It's worked out that way. I didn't have space for a live-in housekeeper and I didn't want to spring a new home on Becca when she was already familiar with this place." He sipped his drink, his brow knit. "Plus, I wasn't in any state to make buying and selling decisions."

"I can appreciate that." Soon after Joey's birth she'd been asked to make some major decisions concerning her son's life and her own. Difficult under the best of circumstances; impossible under the worst.

Her eyes had gone sad again, Sam noted. He couldn't bear that. He dealt with people going through grief and loss every day, yet with Megan it seemed much more personal. He didn't analyze, just set his glass on the coffee table and leaned toward her. Her breath rushed out. Her mouth was only a whisper away. Too far away. Longing wouldn't be denied.

Megan's eyes widened as she realized his intent. In one movement Sam set her glass next to his and settled his mouth over hers.

Pull away... She needed to...to push...needed to drown in the taste of him. The scent of fresh air and his woodsy cologne surrounded her. The press of his mouth, certain and gentle, coaxed the responses she couldn't hold back.

She sagged into the back of the couch, moaning as he feathered his fingers through her hair. His thumbs caressed each side of her jaw, languorous strokes in rhythm to the movement of his lips over hers. She was floating, swirling on a haze of awakened needs. Needs she'd never felt as keenly as now.

Starting with the need to be held, to be closer to this fire Sam ignited. Somehow he read her mind, because in the next second his solid body pressed against her. His heat enveloped her. She caught his shoulders, glorying in the strength and power under her palms. She held him tightly, her anchor in the tempest raging inside her.

Sam was burning, aching as never before. Megan's sweetness—he would never get enough. She was softness and sexy temptation. He wanted her with an urgency that astounded him. The taste of her swamped him with a desire to ravish, plunder. But he went slowly, testing and teasing, hopefully driving her a little bit insane. Definitely driving himself mad. Her breasts were soft against his chest. He inhaled the apple scent of her hair and knew he would always associate apples with this moment and this woman.

He pulled away to draw in a ragged breath. "Megan. Sweet Megan." He nibbled her earlobe. "I want you so."

She stiffened at his whispered words. Her hands that had held onto him so tightly now pushed at his chest, forcing him an arm's length away. Gone was the dreamy, heated smolder that had lit her eyes when they'd first fluttered open.

"Megan, sweetheart, what is it?"

Megan shook her head. How could she explain her incredible stupidity? "I want you. I want you." How many times had she heard that line and fallen for it, taken it to mean so much more, allowed herself to believe that want and love went hand in hand? She couldn't make that mistake again.

She was out the door, leaving Sam still reeling from the shock.

Chapter Four

Insane. Yes, that was it, Megan decided, pacing her kitchen, too shocked and agitated to be still. She'd lost her mind. Nothing else could explain what she'd just done.

How could she have let Sam kiss her? How could she have kissed him back?

And it hadn't been a demure, friendly kiss, either. She still reeled from wanting more. Wanting him. She'd thrown all of herself into that moment. All her pent-up longings and unfulfilled dreams. All her unfocused energy now had a focus—passion.

Passion and Sam Armstrong. Her strides halted. She groaned aloud. Great going, she scolded herself. In one evening, she'd undone all the progress she'd made this past year. Dealing with the pain. Picking up the pieces and becoming stronger. The resolve to break the patterns of the past. None of that had mattered when she was in Sam's arms.

That enchanting smile of his had worked its magic on her, lulling her into forgetfulness. Thank heaven reality had intruded before she'd gone further. She'd saved herself. Just barely.

She could still feel the warmth of him. Still feel the wonder of his arms around her. She'd wanted to hold on and never let go. Never before had she felt so cherished.

Add in the family situation and it was no wonder she'd lost her head. Being with Sam, putting the children to bed, staying to share a drink and talk at the end of the day. All this had weakened her, made her susceptible to his charms.

Tonight she'd slipped, but it wouldn't happen again, she vowed. They were neighbors and that was all they would ever be. That decided, she went to the bedroom to brush her hair. With each furious stroke she reminded herself of the promise she'd made to herself once Alex had left her. No more attempts at love.

She and Sam would wave to each other as they left for work in the mornings, would speak politely when they spotted each other in their yards—Sam playing with the children, Megan tending her garden....

The garden! Aghast, she dropped the brush on the dresser and stared at her reflection in the mirror. Sam was supposed to till her garden plot. Saturday. She couldn't risk being with him, not even for a short time.

She could change her mind, take cooking classes instead of becoming a gardener. But, no. She wanted the joy of watching things grow. So that left her one day to make other arrangements for getting her project started. Arrangements that didn't include Sam.

Her only contacts outside of the two neighbors she'd met were her new co-workers. The firm employed six C.P.A.s, several junior accountants and various clerical staff. Someone there would be able to lend her a hand with the garden, she decided as she got into bed.

Easier said than done, though, she discovered the next morning. The guys at the office were into racquetball, boating on the area lakes or watching sports on TV. The women focused their energy on aerobics, the PTA or housecleaning around husbands parked on the couch to watch their favorite sports. No one was into dirt under their fingernails.

"Why on earth do you want to grow groceries when there's a perfectly wonderful gourmet place just around the corner from this building?" Liz asked her later that morning.

Liz was twenty-seven, single, bubbly and boisterous. She and Megan had become friends instantly upon Megan's arrival at the firm. But Liz couldn't understand Megan's need to nurture the seedlings as they grew.

"I live in suburbia now, Liz," she said by way of explanation. "So I'm doing as the suburbanites do."

"Well, then, one of your neighbors ought to be able to help you. If you're set on doing this awful thing."

Megan could have screamed in frustration. All her efforts seemed to somehow lead back to the man she was trying to avoid. It was as if Sam were becoming inextricably involved in her life—and that she couldn't allow.

Liz took a moment to study her manicured nails, then headed for the doorway, pausing to glance back at Megan. "Tim's office bought a bunch of tickets to the Royals game tonight, and I know they have extras. Wanna go with us?"

The baseball game. The ballpark was still a family thing, a place where fathers took their kids. Megan wasn't sure how well she could handle that scene, but it was time she stopped running from life.

She swallowed her trepidation and nodded. "Sounds great."

"Good. I'll tell Tim. What are you doing for lunch?"

"Buying furniture for my deck."

Liz groaned. "Don't tell me. You're going to sit there and watch your garden grow." She shuddered. "We've got to get you a man."

As Liz bounced out of the office, Megan sighed. How could she make her friend understand a man was the last thing she wanted? That she'd played at love and lost each time?

To Megan's dismay, Saturday morning dawned beautifully sunny and pleasantly warm. She'd prayed for a deluge, an unbearable heat wave for the weekend, a plague of locusts—anything to prevent Sam's tilling her garden. But Fate had no intention of letting her off the hook.

She wasn't sure her resolve was strong enough to withstand the temptation of being with him. A day and a half hadn't been long enough to squelch the needs he'd awakened, put out the fires he'd kindled.

When he knocked on her back door promptly at nine-thirty that morning, she knew she was in trouble. He stood there, incredibly sexy and undeniably alluring, with Brian in his arms and Becca beside him. When he grinned, it was all Megan could do not to melt under the heat. The memories crowded in, urging her to surrender to her longings.

"We called Mr. Henderson, but he can't watch us today," Becca stated happily.

"Is he all right?" Megan asked, stepping out onto the deck.

Sam nodded. "His daughter's in town. She showed up last night with the kids."

"Oh?" There was a hard edge to his voice that told Megan there was more to the story than a daughter bringing the grandkids for a visit.

"She's apparently left her husband. Jack's pretty upset about it."

Sam's mouth tightened in a grim line. Megan understood his reaction all too well—another example of love not working out. How many of those did he see in his practice? Too many, she guessed, looking at him.

"Then are we still on for my garden?" she asked.

"If you watch us," Becca said, her eyes bright and hopeful.

"We'll understand if you'd rather not," Sam added before she could answer.

He was thinking of her feelings again, Megan realized, giving her an out if she needed it. She felt her resolve weaken, then she looked at Becca and was lost. How could anyone deny this child anything?

"Sure, I'll watch you guys," she said.

Becca let out a cheer. Brian wriggled until Sam set him down. Though he had no idea what the celebration was about, the boy squealed with joy as his sister danced up and down. When Becca stopped, he latched onto Megan's leg and laughed up at her.

She stared down at the little boy so full of affection and a need to have it returned. She couldn't afford these emotions he was arousing. It was so painful to see him and remember the son she'd lost. But Brian had lost the two most important people in his life, and that tugged at her heartstrings. How she longed to gather him close and hold him as she had that night he'd fallen and bumped his mouth.

It would be so easy to give in, so wonderful. But she couldn't allow herself to forget what had followed after she'd carried him to his crib. Being there in his room had felt like coming home.

Sam's house, though, was not her home and she would never be part of his little family.

"Maybe this isn't such a good idea," Sam muttered, trying to pry Brian from Megan's pant legs. The kid was having none of it. He clung to her, determined to hang on.

Sam glanced up at Megan's face, reading her anguish, her sorrow, fear and joy. Brian wanted her, and as much as she wanted to accept his attachment, she couldn't.

Sam wanted to hold her. She looked so alluring in curve-fitting jeans and a mint green T-shirt. So in need of comfort, her expression full of longing and loneliness. He needed to hold her—like never before and with an urgency that shook him to the core.

But he didn't have the right to give in to that need.

"Brian likes Megan best," Becca piped up.

Megan blinked. Brian began to fuss and tug harder on the leg of her jeans, begging her to pick him up. He still refused to come to Sam. Megan reached down and ran a hand through the boy's soft hair. Brian raised his hands up to her. When Sam reached for him, Brian batted his hands away.

With a sigh, Megan bent down and scooped Brian into her arms. Laughing happily, he patted her cheek, then planted a slobbery, wet, warm and wonderful kiss on it. Megan gasped.

"Megan . . ." Sam said helplessly.

She gave him a sad smile. "It's okay." She touched a gentle fingertip to Brian's button nose. "Determined little fella, aren't you?" she asked the boy.

Brian flashed Sam a triumphant smile and babbled loudly, as if announcing who'd won this battle of wills. Sam had the sinking feeling the boy might not be as cooperative as his sister, and that his stubbornness would lead to definite clashes in the future. That issue, though, would have to be dealt with one day at a time. The issue also served as a reminder of Sam's priorities. As much as Megan drew him, he had other obligations.

"Guess we should get this show on the road," he announced. "I'll walk over to Jack's and get the tiller. Will you be all right with them?" he asked Megan.

She breathed deeply, then nodded, though a bit uncertainly. Again Sam experienced the strong desire to pull her into his arms, to give her his comfort and his passion. The last thought jolted through him, suddenly and forcefully. He cleared his throat, ruffled Brian's hair, assured Becca he would be right back, then took off for Jack Henderson's.

Megan knew a moment of panic as Sam left her alone with the two children. She didn't know the first thing about taking care of kids. What if one of them got hurt? She'd hate herself if she was responsible for something happening to either of them.

As she expected, Brian wasn't content to sit on her lap for long. Little boys were inquisitive creatures, and he was no exception. He wanted to be put down to explore. He had to stick his fingers in every tiny gap in the wooden deck flooring, try and fit his head through the railings, test his ability to negotiate the three steps.

With Becca's help, Megan kept him entertained and out of too much trouble. Through her efforts and Becca's chatter, her mind strayed repeatedly to Sam as he worked. He was the main topic of Becca's conversation, beaten out of the number one spot only briefly when the deck furniture was delivered and then once again as she helped Megan decide whether to make tea or lemonade.

Megan marveled at the job he was doing with Brian and Becca. Alex hadn't been keen on having a baby. Kids got in the way, he'd told her. But Sam was very different.

And very sexy, her mind added as her glance again strayed toward him. In the warm midmorning sunshine he'd taken off his shirt. The view tempted and tormented her already weak resolve to stay detached. She played with Becca and Brian, but she managed to keep Sam in her line of vision, to observe him working, to wonder and wish.

Physical perfection combined with kindness and caring. The last called to her as much as his virility. Sam was nothing like the self-absorbed men she'd dated, nothing like her ex-husband. It would be so easy to let herself dream of a relationship with him.

Babbling, Brian pulled himself up on her chair and batted her on her leg, as if to scold her for her out-of-line musing. She had no right to think of Sam in those terms. He was a natural father. A man with so much love for children would one day want babies of his own. Megan would have to be content with gardening.

"Hey, what's a hardworking guy got to do to get some of that lemonade?"

Megan started as Sam plopped down next to her on the deck step. Sweat dotted his forehead, trickled from his temples and dripped onto his chest. The sight of it filled her vision, made her breath catch.

She forced her gaze upward, but that grin of his captured her imagination as effectively as his tanned torso. How could her mind hold so many wayward and erotic thoughts? Mental pictures of being held next to his warmth, feeling his heat…his firm, hard body…laughing with him…loving…

"Tax codes," she murmured.

His eyes widened. "I have to recite them to get a drink?"

Megan gasped. She hadn't meant to say the words aloud. They were a distraction, something to correct the course her thoughts had plotted for themselves. "Never mind," she said, shaking her head. "I'll get your lemonade."

"I'll pour it," Becca offered. "Can I? Oh, no. I forgot the pitcher's glass."

"I'll pour, you carry." Megan needed activity, distance from Sam.

She filled a glass and gave it to Becca, watching as the girl very carefully carried the lemonade to her uncle. There was such a bond between them. Sam held her by his side, one arm around her waist in a light hug, as he all but drained the glass in one thirsty gulp. Watching the pair, Megan had to blink back the emotion that swamped her.

Then Brian crawled over to demand his share of Sam's attention and a drink out of Sam's glass. Smiling indulgently, Sam and Becca widened their embrace to include him. Once Brian finished that last swallow of the lemonade, he waved his hands and fussed. Megan carried over the cup he'd been drinking from, but he refused it.

"That's usually a sign he's hungry," Sam said with a tiny sigh.

He'd been hoping for a few more moments to rest before he had to take the kids home and get lunch for them, Megan realized. But resting was a luxury of the past for him, she would bet as the boy's fussing increased in volume and intensity.

"You're tired," she said to Sam. "Let me fix lunch for all of you."

Becca cheered. "We can eat outside on the new table."

Sam's brow rose. "Are you sure?" he asked.

"Consider it a trade-off for the work you've done." She glanced at the fussy toddler. "That is if I have anything Brian can eat."

"You don't have to worry about him," Sam assured her. "He can eat almost everything, and he's not the least bit particular."

"Yeah. He even eats paper and dirt." Becca made a face. "Yuck."

"Double yuck." Sam lifted the boy high over his head and made airplane noises. Brian giggled. "This won't distract him for long," Sam warned between flybys.

Megan took the hint. She and Becca went inside to rummage through the refrigerator's contents. Megan pulled out lean deli turkey, lettuce, tomato and pasta salad, then opened a bag of pretzels. She gave the bag to Becca to take outside, hoping a few munchies would pacify Brian while she carried the bread and sandwich fixings outside.

Lunch was a cozy affair. A bit too cozy for comfort, Sam thought, sitting across from Megan. Being even this close to her was torture. She was so beautiful, the light breeze softly teasing her rich brown hair. Her laughter was sweet music to his starved soul. He longed for the chance to explore the attraction between them.

It was mutual, if her response to his kiss the other night was anything to judge by. He wanted to kiss her again, to make love to her. But that wouldn't be right when he could give her little in return. She wasn't the type of person for a casual fling, he'd decided after she'd run out of his house Thursday night. She should be wooed, romanced with flowers, candlelight dinners, long evening walks. Right now he couldn't give her any of that.

"Thanks for getting the garden tilled," Megan said, relaxing back in her chair and glancing over the straight even rows he'd made in the earth. "You're quite good with that machine."

"Lots of experience helping Jack."

As he finished wiping Brian's face, Megan felt temptation tapping on her shoulder, breathing down her neck, making her want the very thing she couldn't have. She busied herself stacking the paper plates and closing the containers that held the few remains of their impromptu lunch.

"Look," Becca exclaimed, pointing to a little girl who'd come to stand just outside the fence. "Francie has a new bike. Can I go play?"

Sam nodded. "Stay on this block if you go riding."

"Okay. Thank you for lunch. Excuse me from the table. Bye."

Megan laughed at the girl dashing off the list of polite things she'd been taught to say while running to join her friend. "Such manners," she commented.

"Yep." Sam helped Brian out of the chair and set him on the deck. "She managed to get in everything she's supposed to say. Now if I could just get her to say it all while standing still."

Megan couldn't miss the love in his voice. "The kids are very lucky to have you," she mused aloud.

Sam smiled fondly. "It works both ways. Most of the time, at least."

Brian babbled his agreement, then crawled over to the chaise lounge and scrambled up onto it. Once he was sure he was securely seated, he clapped his hands.

"Pretty proud of yourself, aren't you?" Sam asked the boy who grinned once, popped his thumb into his mouth, then dropped backward onto the thick cushion. "I don't believe it," Sam uttered in quiet amazement. "I think he's going to crash."

"I take it he hasn't done much of that lately."

"Not nearly enough to suit either one of us. Last night was another of those nights his teeth kept him awake. I ought to get him home and in his bed, but if I pick him up, he'll start fussing and I'll probably never get him back to sleep."

"Then let him stay there." She shrugged when he trained his gaze on her. "It's sunny and not very windy and where he's lying, the chair's arms will keep him from falling off."

Sam studied the sad and wistful expression on her face and felt it tug at his sympathies. "Megan . . . is it hard for you . . . being around Brian?"

She glanced over at the sleeping boy. "Yeah. It is." She sighed. "But it's . . . well, it's made me realize that I've been putting off dealing with some things."

"Your son's death?"

"Things related to it. Back in Boston, I'd quit going out, especially if I thought there might be kids around. My friends with children were afraid to call or come by for fear that they would upset me. It was easier to let the friendships go than to deal with the pity I saw in their eyes when they looked at me."

"We all do what we have to in order to get by."

She nodded. "For months, I just went through the motions of living. I went back to work when the doctor released me. I came home every night and tried not to think about how empty the house was. . . . Tried not to think at all." She stopped, those painful memories still very fresh.

"What made you pull out of it?"

"I don't know. One night I came home and I couldn't stand the emptiness anymore. I wanted to call a friend, but . . ." She sighed again. "I've changed . . . a lot. It just wasn't the same. So I left it all behind." Left all that had been familiar, everything that reminded her of her folly and her loss. She'd run.

"What about your family?" he asked.

"There was just my parents. They live in Baltimore."

"That's not far from Boston. Didn't they come and stay with you until you got back on your feet?"

Megan shook her head. "Dad's a drug rep. He drives all day. Once he gets home, he likes to sit in his favorite chair, put his feet up and watch TV. Mom doesn't drive."

"Not at all?" Sam asked, his eyebrow raised in disbelief.

"Very seldom. The traffic drives her crazy and finding a place to park frustrates her to no end, so she just takes a cab. It would have to be an emergency for her to get behind the wheel."

"And what you were going through wasn't an emergency?" Sam's brows knit angrily.

"Take it easy on them, Dr. Armstrong," she chided with a small smile—and a warm glow at the way he'd become her champion. "They were there. At least at first, but I kept pushing them away. Then, too, they're firm believers that when you're down, you pull yourself up by your bootstraps—"

"It isn't always that simple."

"So I discovered. But they figured I would bounce back more quickly if I was on my own. They were rather impatient with me when it didn't work out that way."

"Sensitive and caring people generally take longer to heal."

Megan savored the words. "Thanks. I think I really needed to hear that from someone." From someone sensitive and caring. From him. Her feelings were getting out of hand, but she couldn't stop them. "What about you? How did you deal with your sister's death?"

He let out a heavy sigh. "I discovered how much easier it is to be objective about tragedy and to keep things in perspective when it's not personal."

"And when you don't inherit two children so suddenly?"

His gaze traveled to little Brian, sleeping on the chaise lounge, his small body curled up, his thumb in his mouth.

"I hardly had time to grieve for Nancy and Jeff. I had to find a housekeeper, a school for Becca and turn my house into a home for her and her brother."

"They needed someone, and you were there." It couldn't have been easy for him, fitting two small children into a bachelor life-style. But he hadn't bailed out when the going got rough as Alex had.

"What they needed was their mom and dad. I was a pretty poor substitute at first. Especially as far as Brian was concerned. He knew me, but how do you help a kid Brian's age understand death? He can't even understand why he has to take a bath."

"You do it with a lot of love and patience," Megan stated. "Just the way you've done it."

Sam smiled wryly. "You make me sound like a saint, but I guarantee there were times . . . Especially now that the little stinker is teething."

"Had an unsaintly thought or two, did you?"

"Something along the lines of surgically getting those teeth in, or maybe sedating us both until he's over this."

They both laughed. There was something wonderful in the moment, and something unsettling. Megan felt it keenly. It was there in the easy way they'd shared their feelings— about loss and surviving teething. Sitting there in the warm April sunshine, she felt a connection with Sam. Like warmth after a long cold spell, or water after months of drought, it made the moment more precious.

Perhaps that was why a few minutes later, when Sam asked her to go to the movies with him that night, she agreed without a thought other than how much she wanted to be with him.

Chapter Five

"Uh, Sam…"

She was going to back out of their evening as quickly as she'd agreed to it, Sam realized. He could see her searching for words to tell him she couldn't go with him. He should let her, before he lived to regret his impulsiveness, but he wanted her company—enough that he would go against his cautious nature just to be with her.

"Two friends going to see a movie," he rushed to say. "That's all it'll be."

She shot him a skeptical glance.

"Really," he told her with all the sincerity he could muster when what he truly wanted was what he couldn't have. To get to know her. Thoroughly. Intimately. "My life's been in such turmoil since the kids came to live with me. And as far as friendships go, like yours, many of mine didn't survive the changes in my life-style."

That made Megan hesitate. He appreciated firsthand what she'd gone through, and she sympathized with what he was going through. Sympathized much too easily. Why was her heart so soft, and always when she needed to be strong? She'd made so many mistakes where men and relationships were concerned, and she was very afraid of making another.

"I don't know, Sam..."

He glanced again at his sleeping nephew, then back to her. Megan sensed he was sorting through his thoughts.

"Megan, you have to know I find you attractive, especially after the way I kissed you—"

She stiffened, knowing she needed to be wary where this man was concerned, knowing, too, how very difficult that was for her. "I'm not looking for a relationship."

"I guessed as much when you ran out of the house, without a word. I did wonder why, though. I mean, I know my skills have gotten rusty, but I didn't think I was so bad I sent you running."

No, she'd fled because it had felt so good to be kissed by him, so right to stay. Unbelievably right. More so than with any other man. She'd wanted to surrender completely. Only at the last moment had she thought of the danger.

She breathed deeply and exhaled slowly. "My husband. He took off when..."

"When your son died?" he prompted gently when her silence dragged on.

So much had died with Joey—hope, trust and a whole lot of dreams—and that had devastated her to the core. Megan closed her eyes against the anger and pain those memories still carried. "Alex filed for divorce the day I got home from the hospital."

Sam swore softly. "Of all the insensitive... You needed someone, him, to be there for you and he ran out."

Megan marveled at Sam's sympathy and compassion. His understanding. He was so easy to confide in. She needed a confidant, someone to hold her, and it had felt good to have Sam hold her. If only she could trust him, trust her own judgment. But courtesy of Alex, she'd learned how steep the price for mistakes could be.

"I guess," Sam continued slowly, "I just wanted you to know that... Well, I wanted to say I'm sorry for kissing you."

Her brow shot up in surprise. Sam also noted a touch of hurt in her eyes.

"I meant that I was moving way too fast," he rushed to explain. He just hadn't been able to hold his curiosity about how she would taste and how she would feel pressed against him in check. Longings had taken him by storm, demanding action. So he'd kissed her. And he'd liked it. A lot. Wanted more, despite all the reasons against wanting.

"I had no right to do it," he continued. "Not with my circumstances being what they are. Since I've inherited these two munchkins, I've had to cut back on everything, my practice included, and still some days I don't have a spare moment to catch my breath."

"Or do other things. I haven't seen you running in the mornings," she said quietly.

"You noticed?" His wry grin turned mischievous when she blushed ever so slightly. She'd been watching him, he thought with pleasure. "Brian's been awake so much at night that I haven't been getting up early enough to run before going to the hospital. I've been trying to get in twenty or thirty minutes at lunch whenever my schedule is free."

"Kids do have a way of rearranging your priorities." Even planning for a child had changed her life and her ways of looking at things, she'd found.

He nodded. "The point I'm trying to make is that I know relationships take a lot of time and nurturing and that I don't have much time to invest in one. Serious or otherwise. And with my present circumstances, one of which is crashed on your new deck furniture, it wouldn't be fair to ask you for a date, per se."

"But a movie—"

"Two friends. One who desperately needs an evening off. One who maybe could use an evening out?"

When he smiled, Megan knew there was no way she could turn him down. They'd both been through a lot. Were trying to establish a new status quo out of the chaos of their lives. They each needed someone to talk to, someone who understood.

"All right, Sam," she said. "What time do you want to leave?"

"How about six-thirty? I don't think I could get away for dinner since I'll be calling the sitter at the last minute and all."

"That's fine." Better, in fact, Megan wanted to say. She wasn't ready for dinner with him. Though this trip to the movies wasn't really a date, it sure felt uncomfortably similar to one.

Five-thirty and still no sitter. Sam hung up the phone for the seventh time and glared at it long and hard. There wasn't a teenage girl in the city—at least not one he knew and trusted—who didn't already have plans this Saturday night.

So what was he going to do? He wanted this evening out with Megan with a desperation that should have him worried. But the only thing worrying him was how to manage it.

"Who's gonna stay wif us?" Becca asked plaintively, slipping into her baby talk. A sure sign she was worried about his leaving.

Sam pulled her onto his lap. They went through this every time he went out. She still remembered the night her mommy and daddy didn't come home to her and her little brother. So Sam went out often, though usually it was only over to Jack Henderson's for a quick beer—just to reinforce in Becca's mind that what happened to her mom and dad was not the norm.

"I don't know, sweetheart," he said, hugging the girl tightly. "Everyone's busy tonight." Prom weekend at the nearby high school.

"Then you hafta stay home."

This time I really need a break, Sam longed to say. But Becca was too young to understand his needs and just old enough to get her feelings hurt at the thought he might find her a burden. Sam wouldn't let her think that for the world.

"But I promised Megan I'd take her to the movies." He stared at his list of sitters as if he would miraculously find the name of someone who hadn't already turned him down, someone trustworthy and looking for a few hours' pay.

"Then I guess..." Becca sighed heavily. "I guess you could call Emmaline," she suggested in a very tiny voice that made Sam suspect she was holding back some important information she should have given him before now.

"Emmaline?" he asked.

Becca nodded. "A long time ago she said for me to tell you she knows a girl named Jill who could baby-sit us sometimes."

"And you didn't pass this on to me before now because you wanted me to stay home with you?"

Her lower lip pouted.

Sam's heart ached for his little niece. He was all she had now and she was so afraid of losing him, too. "So why are you telling me now?" he asked softly, his mouth pressed against her tiny ear.

"'Cuz you promised Megan."

Chuckling, he hugged her tighter. "Then for Megan you'll let me go out tonight. Why is that?"

"Becuz she likes me and 'cuz she smells pretty."

That she did. Like apple blossoms and wildflowers. Sam didn't think he would ever get enough of her sweet scent. He only wished he had the right to tell her.

"Okay, Munchkin Princess," he said, kissing the top of Becca's head as he reached for the phone. "Let's hope this Jill is dependable and available."

With Emmaline's praise of Jill and his own impression of the girl, Sam was satisfied he was leaving his two charges in good hands for the evening. He showered and dressed in record time, but still didn't manage to make it out of the house on schedule. As he rang Megan's doorbell, he peered anxiously at his watch.

"Sorry I'm late," he told her when she opened the door.

Years too late, he thought as she stepped onto the porch and stood beside him. She wore black stretch leggings and an oversized pale blue silk shirt that outlined the curve of her breasts temptingly.

If only they'd met before he'd inherited so much added responsibility, back in the days when he had the time to romance a woman the way she should be romanced. When he had the time to get to know her and she wasn't recovering from the double whammy of divorce and her infant son's death.

"You look a little frazzled," Megan commented when Sam settled her into his sports car at just before seven o'clock. She had to squelch the longing to run her hand over his brow and smooth away the wrinkles of worry and frustration. Feelings she shouldn't be entertaining at all.

"The best laid plans mean nothing to a cranky ten-month-old." He laughed wryly. "Over the course of my practice, I've had several single parents as patients. 'Get out. Meet someone you can talk to. Date.' That's been my standard answer. Boy am I finding out just how pat an answer that is when there are little kids involved.''

"There are plenty of people who manage kids and a social life successfully.'' Megan supplied this observation helpfully.

Sam groaned. "It's such a hassle finding a sitter. I either have to find one whose parents can drive her to the house and pick her up, or I pack both kids in the car and drive both ways. Brian definitely resents having his sleep interrupted.''

"That is rough, but at least Becca is old enough to help you some.''

"Not as far as my socializing is concerned.'' He sighed. "She's so afraid history is going to repeat itself with me. And all the while I'm gone, I have to deal with knowing how really scared she is that I won't come back.''

"I couldn't imagine how hard that would be. But you have to have a social life. And she has to learn that people leave and they do come back.''

"Yeah. I know one day she will get over her fears.''

Megan nodded. "Until then, though, there's this neat frozen yogurt place across from the theaters. I've only been there once, but they happened to be handing out samples. Everything tasted great.'' As he pulled into the parking lot, she pointed to the little strip mall across the street. "There it is. It's open late on Friday and Saturday nights. We could stop in after the movie and take something back to her.''

Sam glanced at her in surprise. "You wouldn't mind going home as soon as the movie's over?''

She shook her head.

She was one amazing woman, he thought as he parked the car, then walked her into the theater. She put a little girl's needs before her own pleasure. The women he'd been dating when Becca and Brian first came to live with him hadn't been that understanding and thoughtful.

Because of Sam's trouble finding a sitter, he and Megan were arriving just as the movie was starting. They found a pair of seats on the side aisle and settled in. But with all his need for something to take his mind off the trials of parenthood for a while, Sam found himself hardly paying attention to the film.

By mutual agreement they'd chosen an action flick, purposely avoiding the romantic comedy and psychological thriller. The film was good—the parts he noticed, at least. But Megan was a constant distraction. Her scent, fresh and flowery, wafted around him, teasing his senses. The warmth of her next to him tempted and tortured.

Sitting this close to her also made him realize what was missing from his life. Not that he didn't have a lot to enjoy and be thankful for. He did. But every now and then he longed for someone to walk the floors with him, someone to talk to in the quiet of the night, another hand to hold and share the load.

Megan understood what he was going through. He was coming to realize how warm and caring she was, how much he could come to care for her. He still remembered the kiss they'd shared. Recalled it vividly. Passion and promise. But he would have to be content with so much less than he wanted. He couldn't chance that things wouldn't work out between them and she or the kids would be hurt.

Megan shifted in her seat. As hard as she tried, she couldn't concentrate on the movie. Sam was too close and she was too aware of him. She wanted to lean into his solid strength, not to take comfort, but rather to offer it. She sensed the sleepless nights and responsibilities weighed on him a little more heavily than usual.

He'd given her so much in the few days they'd been neighbors. His help. His shoulder to cry on. Space when she asked for it. His understanding and compassion. What could it hurt to give him just a little more of herself to ease the strain he was under?

She slid her hand into his. He stiffened momentarily in surprise, then his strong fingers closed tightly over hers. A jolt of awareness shot through her. She worked to control the longing that raced through her. He was virile and vital and she'd been craving this kind of contact with him from the first time he'd held her.

But this was all there could ever be between them—a fragile friendship. As she sensed him relaxing a bit, she closed her eyes to savor the feel of his hand around hers. This was what she needed. She would take all she could from the moment.

Too soon it was over, they were exiting the theater and Sam was helping her into his car. She'd thought the feeling of connecting with him would vanish outside the intimacy of the dark theater. To her surprise and pleasure, the feeling lingered. It felt very natural when his arm brushed hers as he put the key into the ignition.

"This car was not manufactured with marriage and a family in mind," she commented dryly.

He chuckled. "Yeah. I bought it two years ago. Back in the days when I was totally on my own and still liked to drive with the sunroof open, the radio loud on the easy rock station and my mind on who I could sucker into a racquetball game after my last patient."

Megan laughed. "The good old days, you mean."

"Exactly."

She studied his profile as he maneuvered the car through the theater traffic and across the busy street to the Yogurt Shoppe. His jaw was more relaxed, the lines of his brow smoother, his smile full of genuine mirth. The evening out had refreshed his spirit. Hers, too, she realized. She felt renewed, happy. Things she hadn't felt in a long time.

It was very good to laugh, to be carefree and with someone whose company she truly enjoyed. She would forget about worries over what the future held for them. For now there was just her and Sam.

So she found herself pointing out the yogurt flavors she loved and asking Sam which he thought Becca would enjoy. In the end she chose two flavors and had them packed in one-pint containers. Megan even treated.

"You're spoiling her," Sam told her as they got back in the car.

"Look at the potential psychological advantages," she insisted. "Becca will begin to associate good things with your going out."

He switched on the radio and turned up the volume as they drove back to the house. He even opened the sunroof when Megan laughingly mentioned it. She relaxed in the bucket seat as he drove through the date-night traffic.

At home, he insisted she take the yogurt in to Becca. "You bought, you present," he dictated.

"And if she comes to associate good things only with your going out with me, what will you do?"

He leaned close, his face only inches away. His dimple deepened impishly.

"Go out with you," he said. "Very often."

A wonderful thought, she decided as he leaned closer for just an instant. To be with him, near enough to be kissed by... She yanked her wayward thoughts back in line. To be his friend, she amended. But she could really get to where she looked forward to their time together.

"You're home!" Becca shouted, bursting through the door as they walked up the stairs and onto the porch.

Sam scooped her up and kissed her loudly. He opened the door for Megan, then inside, set Becca back on her feet.

"Megan brought you a surprise," he told the girl once he'd paid Jill and her parents had come to get her.

Megan held out the containers, smiling to see the girl's eyes widen with joy. Becca wanted some of each flavor—because she wouldn't be able to sleep from wondering what the second flavor tasted like, and in the morning she would be watching the clock and driving Sam crazy until he said it was time to open the second carton.

Rolling his eyes at her exaggeration and pretty good attempt at manipulation, Sam gave in.

"Kids learn fast," he said to Megan once his niece was busy devouring the treat.

"It was only for an extra scoop of yogurt," Megan said pointedly.

"But one day she'll be testing me on curfew and how short she can wear her skirts."

Megan nodded thoughtfully. Life changed. Children grew. Adults grew older. Nothing stayed the same. And that would include her friendship with Sam. The circumstances of their lives would one day be different. Would there be a place for her in his life?

Becca jumped down from her chair at Sam's kitchen table. "I'm done," she announced.

Sam helped her with washing her face, brushing her teeth and combing her hair, but Megan was drafted into reading the bedtime story—the little book she'd given Becca.

The girl cuddled close to Megan's side in her small bed while Sam watched from the doorway. Megan savored the scene, the warm glow it gave her to hear Becca laugh at her silly rhymes and see her trace her pudgy finger over the drawings she'd made so long ago.

The reminder that she would never have a child of her own hit her again. Fate had stolen that from her. But this time the sorrow was tempered with the knowledge that she could have this moment with Becca. A moment she could treasure. New memories she could take with her. There was a kiss on the cheek and a hug around the neck for her and for Sam, then he turned out the lights and walked Megan back to her own dark house.

The evening air was fresh and fragrant with the budding trees and new grass emerging after the winter's cold. The light of the stars was eclipsed by the brightness of the full moon that shone down on her and Sam.

"Thank you for going out with me tonight," he said as they reached her front door.

"I enjoyed it." Very much. She didn't want the evening to end. Not yet. "Sam," she said slowly, "have you ever thought of... getting married...? I mean..."

"For the kids?" he asked as she searched for words to frame her question. "I'd thought about it. A lot at first. It was all so overwhelming."

"I can imagine."

"My whole life changed in the blink of an eye. The relationships I was in—friends and, well, the women I was dating... Suddenly almost everyone I knew stopped taking my calls or had other things to do when I asked them out."

"They didn't like children?" Megan asked, puzzled. She couldn't see him associating with anyone so different from himself.

He shrugged. "They weren't ready for a family. One in particular—Kristen—told me she felt I was rushing things between us just to find a mother for the kids."

"Was she right?"

"Maybe a little. The kids had lost both parents, and I felt they needed more than an uncle who knew a lot about doting on them and nothing about taking care of them." He chuckled wryly. "It took me weeks just to figure out how to work Becca's hair barrettes."

"Yet you learned."

"Yeah, I did. But what Kristen said made me rethink what I was doing. The kids and I were—are still—undergoing a major adjustment getting used to each other. That's enough to ask them to handle. So for the time being, we'll stumble along on our own."

One day, though, he would start thinking of a relationship, Megan knew. Where would that leave the two of them? Would she get attached to him only to lose him? The thought made her ache inside. Already she could feel the pain of seeing him with another woman. How had she become this attached to him, especially when she'd worked so hard to prevent it?

"How about you?" Sam asked as she unlocked her door. "What does the future hold in the way of relationships for Megan McAllister?" He wasn't sure he wanted to hear the answer, but the question wouldn't be denied. Now that she'd brought up the subject, he had to know if she would ever consider a serious relationship. But the mental picture of her with another man didn't sit right.

"I guess I'm not ready to think about that yet. When Alex left . . . Well, it was very hard for me to deal with."

Sam's jaw tightened. He could have smashed this Alex's face in for the terrible pain he'd caused Megan. Sam didn't even pause to consider the extent of the rage he felt against her ex-husband. "The jerk couldn't have picked a worse time."

Megan nodded. "The really devastating part was finding out that he never loved me, not the way I thought. I thought he would always be there for me, but when I needed some-

one to lean on, he didn't want to deal with the problems."
She sighed. "I'd misread him completely."

"It happens. We think we know someone, then a crisis
proves us wrong."

How well did she know him? she wondered. He'd shown
her more consideration and had given her more of his caring than Alex ever had. But then there'd been no crisis....
It shouldn't matter whether Sam would be there for her,
whether he could take on one more of her problems on top
of his own. She didn't have the right to be thinking of him
in those terms.

"Well," she said, pushing open her front door, "I guess
it's getting late..."

"Yeah, you're right. I don't like to leave the kids alone
too long."

In the moonlight Sam looked down at her lovely face. The
breeze lightly blew her soft hair. A touch of wariness and a
touch of wistfulness lit her eyes. How much he wanted to
hold her, pull her close to him and keep her there. But the
circumstances, the timing... If only he had the freedom to
explore all he felt for her.

On impulse he leaned down and kissed her on the cheek.
Her breath rushed out in surprise. Her eyes widened. She
should be reminding him of his priorities, but there was only
longing in her eyes. Longing nearly as strong as his own.
Longing neither of them could give in to. He gazed down at
her once more, filling his memory with the way she looked
in the moonlight, then he left.

Megan watched him walk across her lawn, his hands deep
in his pockets. She could still feel the warmth of his mouth
against her skin, could still feel it as she got into bed and
turned off the lights. It was a long time before she fell asleep.

Chapter Six

Megan barely noticed the breeze blowing the pages of the landscaping magazine that lay open on her lap. She'd taken the magazine and her coffee out onto the deck early that morning, but her coffee had sat untouched until it had gone cold and she'd soon abandoned her halfhearted attempts to decide on flower boxes for the deck.

She'd dreamed about Sam all night. Because of that tiny kiss on the cheek he'd given her, her head had been filled with visions of the two of them. Laughing. Loving. Then there'd been children. Becca. Brian already preschool age. And other children. A girl and a boy, both with Sam's dimples and her eyes. But that could never be.

Sighing, she tried to pull her mind back to the here and now. There was the mid-Sunday-morning sunshine to enjoy and roses to plan for. Azaleas, too. They would require a lot of tending. Perfect for her. The blooms would be fragrant and beautiful and she would enjoy taking care of them.

She would plant the roses in barrels, she decided. One at each corner of the deck. The azaleas would go in the ground, against the house where they would be sheltered.

"There's Megan. Hi, Megan."

Megan raised her head at Becca's excited shout over the fence to her. Becca's friend stood beside her, an eager-faced little girl with wide hazel eyes and straight dark hair.

"What are you doing?" Becca asked.

"Thinking about flowers. What are you and your friend doing this morning?"

The girls exchanged a conspiratorial glance. Francie shook her head and Becca nodded vigorously. Becca took a step toward Megan. Francie hung back. Finally Becca took the other girl's arm and pulled her forward. Megan tried to hide her amused smile and her curiosity. The pair definitely wanted something and Sam's angelic niece was clearly the ringleader. She waited as the girls approached.

"Me and Francie want you to teach us how to make a book," Becca supplied as she and Francie walked up on the deck. Francie nodded shyly.

"Make a book?" Megan repeated, too surprised to worry about correcting grammar.

"Yeah. Like the one you gave me. Uncle Sam said you painted the pictures and made up the words. We want to know how to do that, too."

Speechless, Megan studied the two. How on earth was she supposed to teach two five-year-olds how to draw and rhyme? Did she even want to try? But how could she possibly refuse when the pair looked at her so expectantly?

"I don't know how this will work," she mused aloud.

"Please," Becca begged. "We'll behave real good."

Megan laughed when Francie nodded her agreement. "I was just trying to figure out where we could go to work and whether I have enough supplies. I haven't even looked at the box of stuff I have since—'' Since Joey died. She caught herself before she said the words to Becca. The girl didn't need to be reminded of painful things any more than Megan did.

"She said yes." The little girls jumped up and down, singing in unison.

"*I* said yes," Megan stressed, pointing first to Becca and then to Francie. "But you need to ask your uncle if it's okay and how long you can stay. And you need to ask your mom, Francie."

They were gone before Megan could blink. Grinning at their enthusiasm, she carried her magazine and coffee cup into the house. In the back of her hall storage/linen closet, she found the box of art supplies, dug it out and carried it to the counter that divided the dining room and kitchen.

The box held so many memories. Her very practical parents, who were always bemused and baffled by this creative side of her. College friends who'd puzzled as to why she'd chosen an accounting career over one in education. The baby boy she'd given birth to, who'd battled for life and lost.

Those last memories still hurt, but she now realized the pain was easing a little more each day. Sam was very instrumental in that. With him she'd been able to express her feelings, and he'd shared his with her. He'd commiserated with her and she with him.

The phone's ringing broke into her thoughts. She wasn't terribly surprised to find Sam on the other end of the line. What did surprise her was the crazy things the sound of his voice did to her. It was warm and sexy and a bit harried. But then she could hear that Brian was crying again.

"Have you lost your mind?" he asked her without preamble. "Two five-year-olds and paint?"

"I'm looking forward to it," she replied, aware she truly was anticipating the fun of trying to teach Becca and her friend. It was a good feeling. Cleanup hassles could be dealt with later.

"Okay, if you're really sure..." There was a note of disbelief in his voice. "I told Becca to come home for lunch."

Megan glanced at the clock. "That won't give us much time. How about I make peanut butter and jelly sandwiches?"

That was greeted with an instant of silence. "You have the stuff on hand? You can't mean you actually eat that concoction?"

"Not only eat it, Dr. Armstrong, but I like it."

Somehow she knew he was shuddering. "And to think I vouched for you to Francie's mom." Brian let out a shriek and his crying became angrier and louder. Sam sighed.

"Another one of those days?" she asked sympathetically.

"Mmm. The little stinker woke up about four this morning and hasn't stopped fussing since then."

Her heart went out to Sam. "Why don't you bring him over? Maybe watching Becca and Francie will take his mind off his teeth."

"No. The kid takes so much attention, and Becca feels bad when she can't help me deal with him. She needs a break and some time to be a little girl. Besides, Brian will want to eat the paper and paints and he's not very understanding when I tell him no."

Megan laughed, the sound soft and melodic to Sam's ears. "I forgot about his eating habits," she said. "Maybe later, then, after we're finished for the day."

Sam glanced at the miserable kid, beating his favorite stuffed dog on the carpet. This was apt to last all day, and Sam didn't think he could face toughing it out alone. Being with Megan would be so comforting and vastly more enjoyable than what he was going through now. Besides, if the truth be known, he would give anything for a chance to see her again.

"I'll take you up on that," he said, already thinking about being with her. "I'm going to try to get him to take a nap after awhile. So, say around three?"

"Great."

She sounded as if she meant it, he thought, smiling as he hung up. His grin faded as he turned to Brian, gathered him up and tried to rock him. At times like this, Sam often wondered if Brian was missing his mother.

Sort of like Sam missed Megan? He'd thought of her long after he'd gotten into bed last night, had wondered if she was a cuddly sleeper, if she liked to snuggle in the mornings, if she would enjoy having a shower buddy to scrub her back....

That last question had given him many moments of discomfort until he'd finally fallen into a restless, erotic, dream-filled sleep. This morning, not even Brian's unpleasant temper or all Sam's own mental warnings not to let his libido get carried away had quelled this hunger for her. Had barely brought it under control. He hadn't thought of a woman in such terms and this strongly for quite a while.

Brian's flailing fist connected with his cheek in a solid slap. Sam caught the little hand and kissed it.

"Thanks, buddy," he said softly. "I needed that."

To bring him to his senses, he thought. As it became clear that rocking Brian wasn't helping, he set the kid down.

Megan was off-limits, at least in any capacity beyond that of a friend. Sam wouldn't risk hurting her or either of the kids by rushing into a relationship before all the uncertainties had been ironed out. They'd all been through enough without him adding to it.

Brian slammed his stuffed dog on Sam's knee, jolting Sam's thoughts back to his current troubles. Lunch, he decided, grabbing the kid and carrying him to the kitchen. He'd already tried the remedies Dr. Spock recommended— teething ring, teething biscuits, teething gel. None of it had worked today. Maybe stuffing his mouth with food would keep Brian quiet for a short time.

Smiling, Sam thought of Megan and her PB&J sandwich. He detested the combination. Could hardly stand to look at it. But for Megan...

"Yes, sir, pal," he told Brian as he sat the boy in his high chair. "For her I'd almost be tempted..."

"Mo-Mo," Brian replied through his tears.

"Yep. Almost. Almost indeed."

Megan surveyed the mess on her kitchen floor with a sense of accomplishment. Under her tutelage Francie and Becca had managed some passable trees and flowers—just before Megan had given them permission to go solo. The figures they'd created to fill in the foreground were stick people and barely recognizable pets.

"Are those birds in the sky?" she asked Becca.

"That's my mommy and daddy. They're angels now. Uncle Sam said so." She pointed the end of her paintbrush at some stick figures on the ground. "That's Uncle Sam. He's going to 'dopt me and be my new daddy."

"Really?" was all Megan could say. Sam wanted the children to be his, legally and completely. But then she should have known he wouldn't do this parenting thing halfway.

"And one day when the judge says he can 'dopt me and Brian," Becca continued, "we'll be a real family." She pointed to the two smaller figures in the painting, then at the other larger one. "That's me and Brian, and this is our new mommy. Uncle Sam says maybe someday we'll have one. And more brothers and sisters.''

"Really?" Megan repeated like a stuck record. As she absorbed what Becca was telling her, it hit home more forcefully than before that she could never be part of that scene. Part of Becca's future.

The girl chattered on about this growing family she wanted and how she would have siblings to play with and teach to tie their shoes. With each excited word, Megan's heart sunk more and more.

Becca shouldn't be denied the family she longed for. Megan couldn't be the one to give it to her. So why was that a problem? Megan asked herself. Exactly what was it she wanted?

Sam. She wanted Sam, wanted to explore this attraction between them. Her breath caught at the realization and the strength of her need to get to know him. Intimately.

But that would be a disaster. Hadn't she learned that people changed as circumstances changed? Right now Sam sympathized with her loss, but he didn't know the whole story. How would he feel to learn she couldn't give him the brothers and sisters he'd promised Becca?

She didn't want to know, she decided, helping the girls put away the paints and clean up. She couldn't bear to think of how the light in his eyes would dim when she told him. Couldn't stand to think of hearing him say how much he wanted the one thing she couldn't give him—children of his own.

She wouldn't tell him. There'd be no need to. She wouldn't let these budding feelings for him go further.

"Can I take my picture home and show my mom?" Francie asked as they stuffed the last of the paint-splattered newspapers into the trash.

"Sure, but be careful with it because it's still wet." She handed the girl the paper, noting that the cat's blue fur was already running into the green grass.

Francie rushed to the front door and came to a stop as she looked up at Megan. "Someone has to watch me cross the street."

"You got it," Megan told her.

She stepped out onto the porch, keeping her gaze on the girl until she opened the door of the tan vinyl-sided home across and three doors up. A tall dark-haired woman came out once Francie was inside and waved to Megan. She waved back, thinking that Francie's mother seemed friendly and hoping they'd get a chance to meet each other.

She'd started back inside when a clattering sound made her turn to Sam's porch. He struggled with Brian and all the paraphernalia one needed when traveling with an infant, even if the journey was only next door.

Megan called to Becca and the two of them ran to give him a hand with the things he'd dropped. Becca grabbed the diaper bag. Megan picked up the high chair, but Brian spotted her and nearly jumped out of Sam's arms, reaching for her. Sam caught the high chair and she caught Brian. His eyes were red and his nose was running profusely.

"Is it safe to assume he didn't take a nap?" she asked as Sam passed her his handkerchief.

"Very."

The one word, muttered, and the tight furrow of Sam's brow said it all. He was exhausted, emotionally drained and frustrated enough to scream.

Gently she dabbed the tears from Brian's cheek and wiped his nose. "Is that better?" she asked him softly.

He nodded once, then lay his head on Megan's shoulder and popped his thumb into his mouth.

Sam gaped in astonishment. "How did you do that?"

Becca giggled. "Told you he likes Megan best."

Sam growled, but Becca only laughed at his mock menace and merrily led the way back to Megan's house. Inside, Brian raised his head to survey his new surroundings, spied the stuffed rabbit on the rocking chair and held out a hand toward it. Megan sat him on one knee and the rabbit on the other as she rocked in the big chair. By the time Becca finished showing her uncle the painting she'd made, Brian was asleep.

"I'd pay big bucks to have you do that about four times a day," Sam said on a weary sigh.

"Poor Sam. He's been dealing you a fit."

He nodded. "You and Emmaline are the only ones who can comfort him when his teeth get to bothering him this much. Makes me wonder if he remembers his mom."

"I remember," Becca said softly.

Smiling sympathetically, Sam pulled her onto his lap. "What do you remember, sweetheart?"

"She used to hold Bri all the time. And rock him." She laid her head against her uncle's chest. "And she would sing to him."

"Did he like that?" Megan asked, feeling the pull on her heartstrings harder than ever.

Becca shrugged. "Mostly he'd just spit up on her."

Sam laughed, heard Megan laughing, too. His eyes met hers, their gazes holding for a long moment. There was something about this sharing, this emotional link with her that felt almost...intimate. He took a deep breath and swallowed the strong longing that rushed through him.

"Well, thank heaven Brian's over that stage," Megan said, her smile soft and sensual.

"Yeah." Becca's nose wrinkled in distaste. "Spit-up smells awful."

Megan laughed quietly. She studied the lines of fatigue that etched Sam's brow and the weary set of his mouth. "Before the conversation deteriorates further," she said, "maybe you'd like to leave the two kids here and grab a short nap."

Sam considered that for a long moment. The idea was very tempting, irresistible almost. But in the end he sat on the floor across from the rocker. "I'd really rather be here," he said on a satisfied sigh.

With her. When he was away from her, he was beginning to feel alone, feel all that was missing in his life. Megan. Dangerous thoughts.

"Back in Boston," she began hesitantly, as if she were still tiptoeing around the memories, "I had this friend whose little boy had a lot of trouble with teething. She had a...unique...way of dealing with it."

"Oh? What was it?" Sam would grab at anything that had the slightest chance at making this ordeal easier—even if that something was to wear a string of garlic around his neck to ward off the evil demons of teething.

"Whiskey. She'd pour a large coffee mug, full to the brim. She'd take a sip, then she'd dip her fingertip in the mug and rub a drop of whiskey on the baby's gums."

Sam's brow shot up in shock, but recalling the day's amount of crying, he had to admit the idea had definite merit. "How much did she drink?"

"Very little, really. After three or four swallows, they'd both fall asleep. Sound asleep."

Sam had forgotten what a good night's sleep was. He decided he might try rubbing a few drops of the premium scotch he had at home on the boy's gums if he had trouble sleeping tonight. That small an amount couldn't hurt the kid and if it made the pain go away, what blessed relief that would be. He was busy imagining that bliss when Becca tugged at his shirtfront.

"I'm hungry," she said.

Sam realized he'd barely touched his own lunch, trying to soothe Brian. "Me, too. How about Chinese take-out?"

"Chicken and broccoli!" she exclaimed. "And that racoon stuff."

"Crab rangoon." Sam glanced at Megan, his heart pausing over the warm and wistful smile she had as she gazed on the sleeping infant in her arms. Desire hit him full force, leaving him reeling from the punch. The more he tried to reason away his feelings for her, or put them on hold, the stronger they grew.

"What do you want to eat, Megan?" Becca asked.

"Me? I don't think your uncle intended—"

"Oh, yes, I did," Sam insisted with emphasis. "You've turned my niece into a true artist and soothed my cranky nephew into slumberland, thereby giving me a few moments of peace and pleasant companionship—"

"I'm pleasant," Becca protested.

Sam kissed her forehead. "You're the best. I meant *adult* companionship."

"Oh."

"Right." He tweaked her button nose. "Anyway," he said, his gaze on Megan again, "the least I can do is buy dinner. The Dragon's specialty is General's Chicken. They make it just spicy enough to be tasty."

"Sounds good," she said, smiling at him.

He wanted to kiss her so badly, it was all he could do to keep his desire in check. And it wasn't just a physical wanting, either—that he could keep under control. But when she held Brian so sweetly, gave so much of herself and her time with Becca . . . Megan was generous, caring and still fragile. He wanted to hold her, to give her comfort, his love.

All the things he couldn't do. He had no right. She'd been hurt enough. He wouldn't waltz into her life until he was certain he could dance the entire dance.

He scooted Becca off his lap and stood. From Megan's phone, he called in the order so it would be ready when he arrived.

"I'll go, too," Becca said as he hung up. She turned to Megan. "They always give me extra fortune cookies."

"But maybe Megan will need some help with Brian," Sam said, watching her for any signs of hesitancy.

She looked down at the sleeping boy, then shook her head. "We'll be fine. You won't be gone all that long."

"Half hour, tops."

He placed the diaper bag beside her chair so it would be handy if she needed anything, then spread Brian's blanket out on the floor, just in case she needed to lay him down.

Once they'd left, Megan carefully adjusted the sleeping bundle in her arms and settled back in the rocker. Brian was so peaceful this way. So beautiful. The moment was heart-achingly wonderful.

She thought of her own son. Would his fingers have been long and delicate, or pudgy? Would his hair have had red highlights like hers, or been dark like Alex's? Would he have breezed through teething, or would he have kept her awake nights as Brian did Sam?

Sam. She sighed heavily, thinking of how her feelings for him were getting out of hand. Like a runaway freight train headed straight for a collision with reality. A train she couldn't stop.

What had ever made her think she could have had a nice, easy friendship with Sam? She'd only been fooling herself. She wanted more than friendship. And just as it had in years past, her heart was rushing in, heedless of reason.

Maybe she could ride this train of wanting Sam until it ran out of steam. Would this need wane with the passage of time?

And what about the siblings Sam had promised Becca?

"Where's a crystal ball when you need one?" she asked the stuffed rabbit just before she sat it on the floor.

Brian squirmed a little, then settled back into sleep. Megan inhaled the baby-powder scent of him, absorbed the feel of him in her arms, touched the softness of his skin. Details, each committed to memory.

She was still rocking Brian when Sam returned. A fleeting wish that this could be the family of her own she'd always wanted crossed her heart; then she let it go. Sam and Becca were teaching her that life was to be lived and there was too little time to spend it in regrets.

The two of them set out the multitude of containers on the counter between the kitchen and dining room, calling out what was in each as they pulled them out of the sack. Suddenly there was silence.

"Something wrong?" she asked, puzzled by the quiet.

"You have no kitchen table," Sam said. "I guess we could take everything over to my house."

"Why go to all that trouble?" Megan told him. "We'll have a picnic in the dining room. There's a big plastic tablecloth in the third drawer beside the refrigerator."

He found it with no trouble and very efficiently had their impromptu picnic set up. Brian awakened at the smell of food and demanded his share of the feast—some rice, a few bites of Becca's chicken, a taste of the egg rolls and the jar of baby food Sam had packed in the diaper bag.

Sleep seemed to have improved the boy's mood. He laughed and played his favorite game—Catch Me If You Can. Megan was amazed that he could move so fast on all fours. When Becca chased after him, he squealed with delight and scurried to Megan just before his sister caught up to him. He scrambled into Megan's lap and hid his face against her chest.

Megan held him close, savoring the rapture of having him dash to her to be "saved" from Becca. He was such a precious bundle. But too soon it was time for Sam to take him and Becca home.

"I like eating on the floor," Becca announced as they gathered Brian's things and crammed them back into the diaper bag.

Megan chuckled. "I saw a table I like on sale in the paper. I'm going to look at it tomorrow after work."

"If you decide to buy it, don't pay for the delivery. We can haul it in my van," Sam offered.

"Van? You can't mean that little sports car you drove to the movies."

"It was my mom's van." Becca supplied the answer, giving Megan a goodbye hug and kiss.

"I use it when I'm carting the kids around." He wriggled Brian's shoes back on the boy's feet, grabbed him up, then carried him over to Megan. "I save the 'babemobile' for impressing dates."

Megan burst out laughing. The man was incorrigible, wonderfully warm and sensitive, and too sexy for her senses. He stood close to let Brian lean over to hug and kiss her, and as the little arms wound round her neck, it was Sam's embrace she longed for.

As he bent down to give her a friendly peck on the cheek, it wasn't friendship that lit the depths of his blue eyes. The barely restrained hunger she saw there beckoned her to lose herself in his heat. Only the memories of past mistakes and the hurt that had followed made her hold back.

As he and the kids trooped out and Megan shut the door behind them, she sighed. That freight train was picking up speed and disaster was right around the corner.

Chapter Seven

"So are you coming with us?" Liz asked over lunch Monday.

When no one answered, Megan looked up from her grilled chicken salad. Three pairs of female eyes stared back at her.

She half smiled an apology to her new friends. Today was the first day in weeks the four of them had managed to get away from the office for lunch together. "Sorry. Guess my mind wandered."

To Sam and the small hug and peck on the cheek he'd given her last night. To how wonderful it would be if he could have stayed with her through the night. To how empty the house had seemed without him. She sighed.

"Oh-oh. That sounded suspiciously like a lovesick sigh," Julie said from Megan's left.

"Sure did," Kelly added.

"And check out her expression," Julie observed.

"There's nothing different about my expression," Megan protested.

The other three exchanged glances. "Mooning," they said in unison.

Megan glared at each of them. Their words were hitting a little too close to the truth. "Change the subject."

"Oooh, touchy," Kelly said, grinning.

"Time to back off, ladies," Liz admonished her cohorts, though there wasn't a lot of earnestness in her tone. "Megan isn't ready to divulge her secrets yet, so we'll just have to wait...."

"And watch," the other two added.

The three of them were so blatantly and desperately curious that Megan had to laugh. "With friends like you gals, who needs nosy busybodies!"

They took the comment in the good-natured way it was intended.

"Jeez, Megan, things are getting dull around the office, and now that the tax-season rush has slowed down, we have much more time to pry," Liz said.

"And you do it so well."

Liz beamed at the mock praise. "Practice," she said. "So are we all on for the movies tonight?"

Kelly and Julie voiced their assurances, eyeing Megan when she murmured hers less enthusiastically.

"If you've got a date," Liz said, "we'll understand."

Chuckling at them, Megan pulled a newspaper clipping out of her purse. "This is my date."

"A kitchen table?" Kelly squealed.

Julie leaned over for a glimpse of the clipping. "Nice legs."

Megan grinned. "Thanks. I wanted to see if those limbs looked this good in person."

That earned her a hearty laugh.

"Okay, okay," Liz said, glancing at her watch. "We'll leave from the office, check out this studly table, then hit the theater. It's Kelly's turn to drive."

As much as Megan enjoyed the company of her new friends, she would rather spend the evening with Sam, she realized once she was back at her desk. His smile, warm and sexy, filled her thoughts entirely more than it should and she had no idea what to do about that. She couldn't stand the idea of not having him in her life.

This night out with the girls was just what she needed to regain her perspective. To get her mind to stop conjuring up images of Sam's hard male body entwined with her smaller frame. To get her thinking about someone other than him and something besides being with him, sharing laughter, the hardships and frustration, the feelings.

The thing was, she decided as she finished her work that afternoon and went to meet her girlfriends in the front lobby, she really enjoyed being with Sam. And she was beginning to fear that friendship would never be enough. But anything more was impossible.

She knew all this. Then why, when she bought the table and a couple of end tables for the living room, had she wished Sam was there with her?

And why now, as she sat in the movie theater between Kelly and Liz, did she wish Sam were there beside her?

And why, after she'd argued with herself over these irrational feelings, was she intending to head for Sam's house as soon as the movie was over and Kelly dropped her and the others back at their cars?

Wondering at her sanity once she was behind the wheel, she put the key into the ignition. She should have arranged for the store to deliver the tables. She could still call in the morning and set it up. Do the sensible thing where this relationship with Sam was concerned.

But to her consternation, once she'd parked in front of her garage, she found herself walking over to Sam's house and ringing the doorbell.

She was about to ring it a second time when she heard footsteps. Sam opened the door. When he recognized her, his dimple deepened in a very warm and very inviting smile.

He opened the door wider. "Come in. We're in the middle of the bedtime story. And guess what we're reading?"

Her book. That Becca loved it so much gave Megan a warm glow. "I didn't mean to interrupt—"

"Well, now that you're here, the least you can do is help me." He took her arm in a firm grip and tugged her into the house. "It's your fault I'm in this jam, anyway."

"My fault?" she asked, gazing up into his lively eyes. "And how much of a jam can you get into reading a bedtime story?"

"A lot. I can't come up with a rhyming word for blanket."

Megan began running the word through her mind, but the sudden heat in Sam's eyes quickly short-circuited her thought process. She took a step toward him, drawn like steel to a magnet. His eyes darkened. Her breath caught. His hand came to rest on her shoulder. She felt her resolve melting away.

His mouth met hers, tentative at first, testing, then tasting. In some far-off place, warning bells sounded, but the blood rushing through her ears blocked out the clang. She inhaled the scent of male cologne and baby powder. His warm breath fanned her face, sending tiny shivers of pleasure skittering across her skin.

There was no rush. It was as if she had a lifetime to savor the sensations only Sam could awaken. And his tenderness. She'd never known a man so giving. When he gently pulled her into his embrace, she couldn't stop herself from going.

Didn't even want to try. He cradled her against his hard and unyielding chest. She felt safe, cherished. This was where she belonged and she didn't want to leave.

How could any two people fit together more perfectly? Sam wondered just before he lost all conscious thought. He tasted Megan's sweetness, a nectar with an addicting appeal. He would never get enough.

Her soft curves pressing against him was enough to drive a man crazy with wanting. How long had he craved the feel of her in his arms? And her hunger. He could feel it in the way she trembled against him, hear it in her uneven breathing. Was her pulse racing like his? Her blood pounding through her veins? Her mind reeling with the sensations racking her body?

He was in a place where nothing mattered except the woman in his arms. Then he heard a squeal of delight.

"Megan!"

Reluctantly Sam pulled his mouth from Megan's. Becca charged up to them, came to an abrupt stop and stared up at them.

"Were you guys kissing?" she asked, her curly head inclined, her eyes narrowed and questioning.

"Sort of looks that way," Sam said slowly. What had he done? How the hell could he explain this? He'd pounced on Megan without so much as a by your leave.

Megan breathed deeply. Gone was the wonder of a moment ago, replaced with fear and the certainty her feelings were out of control. And here in Sam's arms was not the place to bring them back in line.

"Can Megan think of a rhyme word for blanket?" Becca queried, oblivious of the sexual tension in the air.

"Yank," Megan said, stunned by how breathless her voice was.

"Yank?" Becca repeated with a thoughtful frown.

"Blanket. Yank it." Which was exactly what Megan needed to do with this irrational desire for Sam Armstrong. But she couldn't begin to do it this close to him.

"Megan..." he began, his voice trembling as much as hers.

"I've got to go." She turned away, but Becca's voice stopped her.

"Aren't you going to tuck me in?"

Megan looked at her, then at Sam. He stood there, so virile, so gentle and understanding, so tempting. Too tempting. The memory of his mouth on hers was too much to handle. It threatened to swamp her senses all over again.

Sam looked into her eyes, studying her, trying to gauge her emotional state. She was shaking. So was he. The kiss had struck a chord and his insides were still humming from the electricity he and Megan generated. She was ready to run for the door, but Sam couldn't let her go. Not like this.

"She'll tuck you in another night, sweetheart," he told Becca, shooing her back to her room, then taking Megan's arm.

"We need to talk about this," he said. "Please. Give me ten minutes, okay?" He waited until she nodded, then let out the breath he'd been holding while he waited for her answer. "There's diet cola in the fridge, if you're thirsty."

Megan wasn't thirsty. She was scared. She paced his living room, all too aware of how weak she was around Sam. She was making another monumental mistake, falling for the wrong man all over again. Sam might not be as self-absorbed as Alex, but he'd told her his life was overfull, overloaded. He didn't have the emotional energy to devote to a relationship right now. She understood, just as she understood there might never be room for her in his life. Not once he knew she couldn't have children.

She couldn't wait there in his living room for him to come out of Becca's room. He would be kind and understanding, and her resolve would collapse like a house of cards in a tiny breeze.

No amount of talking would change that. Though she knew she was being cowardly, immature, not to face him, she had to leave. Her emotions were too unsettled. She let herself out of his house and rushed back to her own.

Sam came into the living room to find Megan gone. Damn! How could he have been so careless and inconsiderate? They'd made an agreement after that last kiss and he'd totally disregarded it. She'd knocked on his door, looking incredibly sexy in that dark red dress with the gold buttons down the front. He'd thought about her all day, wishing he could see her, spend even an hour with her, then when she'd arrived, he'd reacted like a kid, letting his hormones do the thinking.

He'd wanted to whisk her off to bed. To make love to her, slowly and thoroughly, then talk with her long into the night. Even now he wanted to charge over to her house and beg her to let him in so he could tell her how very much he wanted her.

And if things between them didn't last? If the passion cooled and there was nothing left? Rushing into a relationship was a guarantee to a broken heart. He knew. He saw it day after day. Everyone would suffer if he did something foolish. Megan, Becca and Brian—they would all pay the price along with him. Already Becca adored Megan.

Great going, *Doctor,* he snarled under his breath. He'd analyzed the problem, decided the best course, then took the worst one. As if they all hadn't been through enough.

As he picked up some of the evening's clutter of toys, he considered going after Megan. Becca would be asleep soon.

He could walk over to Megan's for a few minutes and they could...talk.

Yeah...right. As if she would believe that. As if she would even let him in. He had asked her to trust him and then he'd blown everything.

Good job, chump, he told himself disgustedly. He dumped the toys in the box and turned out the lights. In bed he closed his eyes, but a vision of Megan—her lips moist from his kiss, her breasts rising with her breathing, her eyes dark with desire, then wide with shock—haunted him.

He soon realized it would be a very long time before he fell asleep and wondered if Megan was having as much trouble finding sleep as he. He hated the thought that what he'd done was keeping her awake. What would he say when he saw her? If he ever did.

What would he do if she never wanted to see him again?

About the fifth or sixth time of Sam's chasing those unpleasant thoughts around, Brian started to fuss. Sam gave it a couple of minutes to see if the boy would find his thumb and go back to sleep, but it was soon clear that wouldn't happen tonight. The fussing quickly escalated to a wail. One that said the boy was in pain.

Sam grabbed his robe and went to get the boy before he woke his sister. As soon as he walked into the room, Sam knew this would be a long night. Brian sat in the crib, his nose running like a spigot on full blast. While he cried, he batted at his ears and kicked his feet. His face was flushed.

Fever and ear infection, Sam would bet. He plucked Brian out of his crib and tried to get a dose of liquid pain reliever down him. He took that and a few sips of water, but he was having none of Sam's taking his temperature.

"Easy. Easy, son. I know you don't like this," he crooned to Brian, "I wouldn't like it, either, but we have to know where we're at on the fever scale."

One-oh-three, he read with alarm.

Damn! What was he supposed to do now? First of all, stay calm, he would have told his patients in the same situation. But now he realized how difficult that was when your child was involved. He was beginning to wonder if he came across to his patients as being sanctimonious. At this moment, he certainly felt that from time to time he must. If everything in life had to have a purpose, then these teething traumas were teaching Sam humility.

And that doctors don't know all the answers.

While he waited for the pain reliever to kick in, he put the boy in a tub of lukewarm water. A bath wasn't what Brian wanted. He wanted to feel better.

But fate decreed that wasn't to happen very soon. For the next two hours, Sam tried everything he could think of to give the boy some comfort. None of the things that worked for last month's ear infection worked this time. All Sam could do was pace the living room and kitchen and croon to the suffering boy.

Brian wasn't interested in any of it. He wanted to feel better and couldn't understand why Sam had to torment him with eardrops, temperature taking, baths, bad-tasting liquid medicine and off-key singing.

Finally Sam decided he couldn't wait until the morning to call the pediatrician. Andy Rossiter would grouch at having his sleep disturbed, but when he saw Brian, he would understand. The boy's fever was up and he was clearly in pain. Sam bypassed Andy's service and called him direct.

Once he'd arranged to meet Andy at the ER, Sam realized he had another problem: What to do about Becca? He didn't want to drag her out of bed. The poor thing had had a bad dream last night and before she could get back to sleep, Brian had started fussing. It had taken a couple of hours to get everyone down for the rest of the night. Becca had been extra slow waking up this morning, though.

Emmaline. He'd call her. He grabbed the phone, then set it down. He couldn't reach her. She was staying with her pregnant daughter who was ready to deliver any day and he didn't have the number.

He turned and cast a scathing glance at the book on the coffee table. Dr. Spock. Sam had found the dog-eared book at Nancy's when he'd collected the kids' things. The text was almost ragged now—evidence of how frequently he'd sought answers to the various child-raising dilemmas. But many times the only response he'd received was an admonishment to trust his instincts.

"I don't think instinct is going to find me someone to sit with your sister," he told the boy as he walked to the living-room window.

Megan's kitchen light was on, he noticed. So she wasn't sleeping, either. Because he'd kissed her?

How could he have behaved so stupidly—to grab what he wanted without a thought to her and the promise he'd made to her? And what was he going to do about it?

He rubbed his jaw tiredly. She'd run out without giving him a chance to apologize and explain. Did that mean she had no desire to listen to his explanation? But he couldn't leave matters in limbo. Whether it was his makeup or his training, he needed resolution. Loose ends just continued to unravel until the cloth was repaired.

Brian raised his head from Sam's shoulder and babbled tearfully, reminding Sam of his appointment with Andy at the ER. He still hadn't found someone to stay with Becca—unless ...

Did he dare ask Megan? Another light went on in her house, as if she'd given up all attempts at sleep. How would she react to this imposition if he did call her?

Slam the phone down in his ear, most likely, and it wouldn't be any more than he deserved. He had to reach her somehow, to beg for a chance to mend what he'd broken. There was no doubt in his mind that their kiss had affected her as much as it had him. Her response had been hot and wildly free and had only fueled his longing for her. But they'd agreed not to pursue that chemistry, and he'd crossed that line.

He looked from his nephew's tearstained face to the phone to the lights on in Megan's house, then back to Brian. Sam felt sure she wouldn't be able to refuse him if the kids were involved. He felt a decidedly guilty twinge at using Brian's illness as a lever to get to Megan, but desperate times and all that...

He picked up the phone and punched out her number, holding his breath while he waited for her to answer. When she did, her voice was hesitant.

"It's Sam," he said, straining for some clue as to how she felt about his middle-of-the-night call.

"Sam... I..."

He had a feeling she was about to tell him to buzz off. He didn't want that, couldn't stand the thought of it, but didn't know what to say. Then Brian began to wail again.

"What... Sam, is something wrong with Brian?"

There was genuine concern in her voice. He tried to ignore the pang of guilt that stabbed his conscience again.

"I think he has an ear infection, a pretty bad one this time," he told her. "He's burning up and hurting so much that I can't let this wait until morning when Emmaline gets here. I need to take him to the ER and—" he took a deep breath, aware this might well be his one and only chance to reach Megan "—I need someone to stay with Becca. I'd try Emmaline, but she's staying with her daughter. I could take Becca with me, but she's sleeping and—"

"Sam," she cut in, "do you have time for all this detailed explanation?"

"No," he replied, grateful that even after the way he'd behaved, she trusted him to not take advantage of her kindness and concern for his small charges.

"Give me five minutes to get dressed."

She'd lost every bit of common sense, Megan thought as she tugged on a pair of sweats and tied her shoes. The man's kisses melted her resistance and heated her insides like no other's ever had.

But this was an emergency. She was doing this for the kids, she told herself and mentally repeated the words like a litany as she walked over to Sam's. He was bundling a screaming Brian and the diaper bag into the van.

"Becca's sound asleep and I left my pager number on the pad beside the phone," he said, getting in behind the wheel.

Megan nodded. He started the engine, put the van in reverse, backed a couple of feet down the driveway, then braked.

"Megan," he called out as she climbed the porch steps.

She paused, then turned toward him.

"When I get back, we'll talk."

She started to refuse. The urge was there. The need to retreat, regroup. These feelings he stirred in her were alarming, intense and unmanageable. But she and Sam had to redraw the boundaries. She nodded and watched him drive off.

As she let herself into his home, she wondered what new boundaries they could set. After that kiss this evening, she'd paced her living room and kitchen, asking herself just what she was going to do.

The trouble was she couldn't make her feelings follow the logic of her head. Whenever she was near Sam, she wanted to give in to desire. And when they were apart, she was thinking about the last time she'd been with him and the next time they would be together.

With a sigh, she plopped on the couch. She was reaching for a magazine on the coffee table when she spotted the ratty copy of a Dr. Spock baby book. Megan held it in her hand, hurting for all she would never have. Then she thought of Sam and smiled at the mental picture of him trying to feel his way through parenthood with help from a learned colleague.

Poor Sam. This change from bachelor to adoptive dad wasn't easy. But Brian and Becca couldn't be in better hands. He was affectionate, kind, caring. He gave of himself so generously. And he was as sexy a man to ever cross her path, Megan's wayward thoughts felt obliged to point out. But it was the other characteristics that made him so hard to resist.

Still, she couldn't let this thing get out of hand—this attraction. She had to protect her heart, and somehow she had to make Sam understand.

After a couple of hours, weary of chasing her musings around in circles, Megan was nearly dozing off. Finally she heard the slam of a car door in the driveway, then a few seconds later, Brian's exhausted sobbing. She went outside to help Sam with all the baby baggage, but when Brian spotted her, he practically propelled himself into her arms.

Sam handed her the boy's blanket and sighed as Brian dropped his head to her shoulder.

"The boy's going to grow up hating doctors," he grumbled. "Me included."

Megan gave him a sympathetic smile. "That rough, huh?"

"Worse." With the diaper bag over his arm, he took Megan's elbow and guided her to the porch steps. "Andy, his pediatrician, examined him and decided his abdomen was tender to the touch.''

Megan gasped a little in alarm. Tender abdomen sounded serious. "But you thought he had an ear infection."

"That was the final diagnosis. He's overworked all those muscles crying his little heart out and they decided that's why he's tender." He walked her inside and locked the door behind them. Running a hand over his eyes, he went on. "Brian's temperature was close to 104 degrees so Andy wanted to rule out other possible problems."

"Oh." Megan was amazed at how she'd tensed in fear at the thought of Brian being seriously ill. She patted the boy's back as he began to whimper again.

"Andy says Brian's ear hurts when he tries to suck his thumb. That's why he's having a hard time going to sleep," Sam explained as the boy fussed a little harder.

"Poor baby," she softly crooned. "Maybe if I rock him for a while..." she murmured.

"Anything you think might help," Sam said earnestly.

She sat in the rocker and adjusted Brian's position so he was cradled tightly in her arms. He had the scent of the hospital on him, reminding her of her own tiny son. She'd so often wished she could have held him this way at least once before he'd died, but he'd been too ill. All she'd been allowed to do was reach in the incubator to hold his little fingers.

"Oh, thank God," Sam whispered as the boy's eyes fluttered closed. "Thank *you*."

Megan glanced up, her gaze colliding with Sam's. Her breath tripped. She saw him swallow hard, but not before she caught the heat in his look.

He cleared his throat quietly. "Can... Uh, can I get you something to drink?"

She shook her head and let her lungs fill again. "Go ahead and get yourself something, though."

"All I want is about a million full-strength Valium and a corner to hide in."

Megan chuckled. "In one evening you've gone from frustrated and frazzled to self-pitying."

Sam's eyebrow started to angle upward, then quickly dropped as if he didn't have the strength to hold it there. He sank onto the couch with a very weary sigh. "Guess I am feeling sorry for myself," he said with a wry smile. "The kid's the one I'm really sorry for. All he wanted was for his ears to quit hurting and his fever to go down, but Andy insisted on blood work, X rays and a catheter urine specimen."

"No wonder you're both worn ragged."

"Mmm."

He closed his eyes briefly. Megan could tell he was struggling to stay awake.

"Maybe I should put him in his bed," she suggested.

Sam blinked his eyes open. "Give him a few more minutes to get really under. If you don't mind—"

He was thinking of Joey, she realized, reading the softness in his eyes. She nodded and settled more deeply into the rocker.

"You never said why you came by earlier tonight," he said after a long moment.

"The table. I ordered it and some end tables. I was going to take you up on your offer to haul them home, but maybe it would be better if—"

"No." He leaned forward, resting his elbows on his knees. "I don't have any excuse for the way I pounced on you earlier—"

"Please, Sam. I understand."

He studied her for a moment, then nodded. "Yeah, I guess you do. We'd be good together."

His gaze was hopeful and there was nothing Megan wanted more than to say yes to him. But if their relationship didn't end now, it was bound to when he learned of her hysterectomy. To think of never kissing him, never being in his arms again, was painful enough. To give her longings a little freedom now would only make parting with Sam later more agonizing.

"I can't," she said, her voice not at all steady.

He nodded once. "You may not want to hear this, but I have to say it. I've never met any woman who could make me want her this badly, and tonight I really felt you wanted me, too. At least for the moment. Was I wrong?"

It would be so easy to lie, but when he looked at her with his soul in his eyes, she couldn't do it. "You weren't wrong, but—" she rushed to insert as she saw the hope rekindled in his gaze "—but there's something you have to know."

He nodded once more and waited.

"When Alex left me..." She breathed deeply and started again. "When he left, well, it made me realize how vulnerable I'd been—how vulnerable anyone in a relationship is. I'm not ready to open myself to that kind of hurt. I'm not sure I ever will be."

"He sure could have timed it better for you, the inconsiderate..." His bitter words trailed off.

"It would have hurt no matter when he told me he was leaving. My whole life revolved around him and the baby I was carrying. I'd let myself believe things would work out, really blinded myself to our problems and his faults. Then when he walked out, it was as if he was telling me that nothing I did was good enough to please him."

"The fault was in him, Megan, not you," Sam said gently.

Stretching, he held out his hand. She placed hers in it, feeling warmth and reassurance in his grip. She squeezed back.

"It took me a long time to get over it," she said.

"And you don't want to give anyone that kind of power over you a second time."

"Exactly." She couldn't tell him the rest. He'd be satisfied with this much, she sensed, and maybe one day soon someone else would come along for him.

Hurt stabbed through her at the thought, but it had to be that way.

"Then if we can't go forward, would you be willing to go backward?" he asked slowly, choosing his words carefully. Now that he understood how fragile she was, he would have an even harder time staying detached. But whatever it took, he would do it. He couldn't stand the thought of losing her completely.

"Backward?"

"Back to being friends. Like we agreed last time. I never should have crossed the line...." Especially when he had the kids and their emotions to consider. Love took time and that wasn't something he had a lot of right now.

"Friends," she repeated as if testing the word.

Then she nodded and smiled at him. Friendship was a lot less than what he wanted, but it was for the best—for all concerned. He would take this little bit and try to be content.

"I think this little guy is really out," Megan said, looking down at the child in her arms. She scooted out of the rocker.

Time to put him to bed, she thought. And she needed some time to herself to figure out why this agreement to remain friends didn't feel quite as satisfactory as it should.

She gently placed the boy in his crib. As she covered him, she took a few minutes to think of Joey and hope that heaven was indeed a truly wonderful place. Then she turned out the lights and pulled the door shut.

She tiptoed back to the living room. Sam was sprawled on the couch—asleep, she realized. She took a long moment to study the strong lines of his handsome face, then let herself out the door.

On the way to her own house, she wondered how she would fill this emptiness inside her.

Chapter Eight

Sam sent her roses. Not the long-stemmed red kind. Not the kind that a florist would deliver. They weren't ones that she could hold in her hand and sniff. Right now they were no more than a piece of paper from the biggest and best nursery in south Kansas City. A gift certificate delivered by special messenger.

"What kind of man sends a woman flowers she has to plant?" Sitting in the chair on the other side of Megan's desk, Liz shuddered. "It's positively sick."

Megan smiled at the gift certificate for six rosebushes. "It's thoughtful." Though she wasn't sure whether he'd chosen the roses instead of mums or some other plant because he somehow knew of her planned garden, or if he'd picked them because roses were a standard. "Sam knows I'm into gardening."

"That's even sicker." Liz shuddered again, harder this time. "Do you know what digging in the dirt does to a manicure? And the insects. Do you have any idea what kind of creepy-crawly things live in dirt? I think I've dated a couple of them."

Megan's grin widened.

"Yeah, well, it was no laughing matter at the time." Liz studied her perfectly groomed nails and sighed. "First gardening, then in a few years you'll be raising a couple of kids and your brain will turn to mush. I'm warning you, all this homemaker stuff will lead you nowhere."

Liz breezed out the door as quickly as she'd breezed in on the delivery man's heels, leaving Megan to ponder her parting words. Liz didn't know Megan couldn't have children of her own. That's how deeply Megan's anguish over the hysterectomy went. As close as she was becoming to Liz, she couldn't share that pain.

But Liz had the nowhere part right. Nowhere was exactly where Megan's feelings for Sam were leading her.

She hadn't been able to clear her mind of the vision of him asleep on the couch last night. He'd looked so tired and worried that her heart had gone out to him. She'd wanted to lie down next to him. Had wanted to kiss him awake, knowing precisely where that would lead.

Sitting at her desk, the chaos of a busy office all around her, she held his gift certificate and dreamed of all the ways she could show her appreciation. She picked up the card that had come with the gift certificate and read it again: "A friend is a forever thing."

Could she handle forever if it meant being only friends with him?

That question plagued her the rest of the day and all the way home from work, and the answer still eluded her as she pulled into her garage a little after seven that evening.

Deciding to take things between them one day at a time, Megan walked over to Sam's. She wanted to thank him for the rosebushes and needed to know how Brian was after last night's episode. She rang the bell and heard Becca's small footsteps running to open the door.

"It's Megan. Hi, Megan. Emmaline, Megan's here!"

A middle-aged woman with graying dark hair came down the hall, carrying Brian on her hip.

"How is he?" Megan asked once she and the housekeeper had introduced themselves.

"He's still a little cranky, but he slept this afternoon."

Brian reached out for her, patting her face when she took him from Emmaline. "Where's your uncle?" she asked. As late as it was, she'd expected him to have been home long ago. And, she acknowledged, she'd been looking forward to seeing him.

"He's working," Becca grumbled.

Emmaline filled in the details. "Dr. Armstrong had an emergency with a patient. He's at the hospital, and we're not sure when he'll be back."

"And I have something to ask him," Becca continued with a pout. "It's important."

"Oh?" Megan prompted.

"He'll give you the same answer he gave you last time," Emmaline warned the girl.

"Maybe not," Becca insisted.

The housekeeper only gave Becca a knowing look.

"What's the question?" Megan asked, untangling Brian's fingers from her hair.

"Can I have one of Francie's puppies?"

"Oh! That's a biggie, all right." Megan cleared her throat. "A dog is a big responsibility."

Becca made a face. "That's what Uncle Sam said."

"Well, he's right. Also, Brian's still pretty small. It would be hard to make him understand that the dog might bite if he pulls its ears or tail."

Becca huffed loudly. "He said that, too."

"Then it sounds as if the answer will probably be no," Megan said gently. Some voice inside her was warning her that she was getting too involved. She couldn't seem to help it. She was getting in deeper and deeper in spite of herself.

"But he can't say no," Becca wailed. "Barker had six puppies and there are three left. Francie's mom said if she doesn't give them away, they have to go to the pound. They put the dogs to sleep there."

"Not every dog," Megan told her. "They can usually find homes for puppies, especially if they're cute."

"They're real cute."

Becca launched into a description of all of them, dwelling on her particular favorite—a female that was brown, white and black, with floppy ears, a tail that wagged all the time and "the bestest smile."

"I didn't know dogs could smile," Megan commented, exchanging a grin with Emmaline.

"This one can," Becca said, beaming. "She's the smartest dog ever. Even Francie's mom says that."

"She would," Emmaline said as the phone rang.

While she went to answer it, Becca continued her list of the puppy's many virtues. She had her sales pitch down pat. Megan guessed Becca had been practicing this list for quite a while. Sam would have the devil of a time refusing.

"Oh, dear." Emmaline hung up, then looked from the phone to the children.

Megan heard the panic in the housekeeper's voice. "What's wrong?"

"My daughter. She's in labor. Oh, dear. I can't call Dr. Armstrong."

"How much time does she have?"

"My son-in-law says Annie's already dilated to six. He said she's had contractions all day and didn't realize it." She looked at the phone again. "I don't know what to do. I want to be with her, but I can't call Dr. Armstrong away from the hospital."

"Megan could watch us," Becca suggested.

"It's not right to impose on her," Emmaline told the girl. "She probably has plans." But there was a hopeful note in her voice.

"No plans," Megan said. "Go. But drive carefully," she said, noting the older woman's anxiety.

Emmaline snatched her purse off the guest closet shelf. "I didn't finish cleaning up after dinner," she said, half to herself and half to Megan. "But the kids have been fed and there's some left over in the oven for the doctor's dinner. You don't think he'll mind my leaving?"

"Go," Megan ordered again. "Dr. Armstrong will understand, I'm sure."

Emmaline smiled. "Of course he will. He said a woman becomes a grandmother for the first time just once in her life. Becca, you help Miss McAllister, you hear?"

"Okay, I will."

Emmaline gave each of the kids a quick kiss, promised Becca she would call as soon as she knew if the baby was a boy or a girl and told Megan to page Sam if there was a problem. Megan assured her they'd be fine and shooed her out the door.

Sam put the car in Park, pausing to glance at the dash clock—nine-fifteen. Man, it had been a long day. He shut off the ignition, then dragged his tired body out of the car and up the porch steps.

With any luck Becca would be ready to tuck in and Brian would already be asleep. *Right, and while you're dreaming, pal, why don't you dream the kid's cut all his molars and is through teething.* He unlocked the door and walked inside, holding his breath at the silence that greeted him. Could the kids possibly be in bed and asleep?

He had to be in the right house, he decided, looking over the toy-littered living room. Then he heard Becca coming quietly down the hall toward him. As always, he was amazed at how adorable she looked, her blond curls tousled after a busy day, the lace on her little cotton nightgown skimming her delicate ankles.

"Emmaline's a grandma now," she said as he picked her up and they hugged tightly.

"A grandma, huh? When did this happen?"

"Just a little while ago. It's a girl baby and I'm going to share my hair bows with her—if that's okay?"

"I think that's a wonderful idea and you're a very thoughtful young lady to want to share."

She giggled and buried her cherubic face in his neck.

"So who did Emmaline get to stay with you and Bri?" he asked, starting down the hall with her still in his arms.

"Megan."

Sam's steps faltered. He didn't know how it had come to pass that she was staying with his children, but he was happy—elated—with this turn of events. The three people he most wanted to see after a long and very hard day.

"She's in Brian's room," Becca told him as he pushed the door to her bedroom open. "Giving him his bottle."

"So that's why he's so quiet."

He breathed deeply to still the pounding of his heart and get his needs for Megan under control as he continued down the hall toward his nephew's room. He wouldn't take any risks. This evening's trip to the hospital to see his patient had made him realize all over again the value of having someone to talk to, to share feelings with. Someone to keep you from feeling so all alone.

He walked to the doorway of Brian's room and came to a stop as desire knifed through him. For that second before she knew he was there, Megan's head was bent and her gaze was soft and warm as she gave her full attention to the baby she held so close.

No woman had ever looked more beautiful. None had ever made him want her as much as he wanted Megan. Is this the way a man felt to see the woman he'd married hold his child?

Then she glanced up and smiled at him. Sam had to drag air into his lungs. For a moment he just stood there, absorbing the sense of family and home, knowing nothing would ever come close to making him feel this complete—an emotion he would savor and analyze later.

Returning her smile, he stepped closer to where she sat in the rocking chair.

"Megan to the rescue again," he said.

Becca giggled. Brian turned his head slightly at the sound. When he saw Sam, his sleepy eyes brightened and he raised his small hand. Sam offered him an index finger. Brian grabbed hold and grinned up at Sam. Rivulets of formula dribbled out of the upturned corners of his mouth.

Megan dabbed at the milk with the edge of the cloth diaper she'd tucked under his chin. The action was so natural, as if she'd fed him often, not for the first time. A natural mother, Sam thought. Then came the mental image of her carrying his child inside her.

Now what the hell was he going to do about that?

Megan glanced into his eyes and saw the blue depths darken with a sudden heat. The warmth drew her, beckoned her to forget danger and come closer to the flame. There was promise and passion and she wanted to grab both and never let go. Oh, how she wanted. More than she'd known she could. She was playing with fire, and there was no way to keep from being burned. She'd do well to remember how she'd led with her heart before and it had cost her everything.

She heard Sam sigh, watched him pull his gaze away, lowering it to Brian. The baby's eyes were drooping shut. Sam gently disengaged his finger.

"I'll tuck Becca in," he said softly so as not to disturb Brian's journey into slumberland.

"I want Megan to do it," she protested in a loud whisper.

"After she puts Bri down, okay?"

She nodded.

As he walked out of the room, Becca in his arms, Megan felt the tug on her heartstrings. That pull was becoming stronger each time she was here, helping with his children. She needed to get her emotions under control, but they were intent on running wild.

It felt too good to care for his children, to put them both in a bubble bath, help Becca into her little nightgown and play-wrestle Brian into his one-piece pajamas. To read Becca a story while giving her brother his bottle.

Then to have Sam come home. If she let herself, she could almost believe this was her small family and he was coming home to her at the end of a long day.

It would be so easy, so very wonderful, so... fruitless.

Back to reality with a jolt. A jolt she needed, she chided herself. Brian's jaws were slack, the empty bottle barely held in his mouth. Megan took it out and gently laid him in his crib, covered him and switched off the light.

Sam was still in Becca's room, sitting beside her as she extolled the virtues of "her" puppy. He listened, but Megan sensed he was ready to deliver a firm negative answer. Becca must have sensed the same thing.

"Tell him how pretty and smart she is," she urged Megan upon seeing her in the doorway.

Sam shot her a curious glance. "We took a little trip to Francie's to see the puppies," she explained. "They were cute, but, Becca, a puppy is an awful lot of work. Your uncle has his hands full now."

Sam smiled gratefully. Becca caught her breath.

"I'll take care of her," she insisted. "Please...you're not going to say no. You can't. Francie's mom said the puppies have to have a home by tomorrow. All of them."

Sam's eyes narrowed in suspicion.

"Seems that while the humans were at the store buying puppy food," Megan said, "the three mongrels ganged up on Helen's new leather shoes, after which one of the pups was sick on the new dining room carpet."

"I'm beginning to get the picture here," Sam said, his eyes narrowed even more.

"That's not all. Two of them went . . . you know. On the new dining room carpet."

"Helen and Ed just put down carpet, I take it," Sam said.

"Right the first time," Megan said with a nod. "And the three puppies ran completely amok on this new carpet, in true, unsupervised puppy fashion."

He sighed and turned to Becca. "Sweetheart—"

"Please don't say no," she begged. "Please say you'll think about it."

"I already have and—"

"Say you'll think about it some more. Please. Please."

She made her eyes fill with ready-to-fall tears and her lower lip pout sorrowfully. Megan heard Sam take a deep breath as if to gather strength for the battle that had to be fought. Then he let the air out slowly, deflating like a balloon with a slow leak. She had to hide her smile as he told his niece he would think about this puppy.

"Didn't have the heart to say no?" she asked once Becca was kissed, covered and the bedroom lights were out.

He draped his arm lightly around Megan's shoulders as he walked her down the hall to the living room. "I didn't hear you telling her no," he said with mock-annoyance.

"Not my fight."

His arm still around her, he walked over to the couch and tugged her to sit beside him. She shouldn't stay, but she couldn't make herself leave when being by his side felt so right; and when she knew that by his side was where she most wanted to be.

"Emmaline left your dinner in the oven," she said, desperately trying to check her runaway longing to lean against his chest.

"I'm not ready for food yet."

When he sighed heavily, Megan looked up. She studied his furrowed brow, his slight frown and the faraway look in his eyes. All of it spoke volumes of his painful thoughts.

"Thinking of your patient?" she asked.

He nodded and sighed. "A young woman. Mother of three. I only started working with her last week. She's the first new patient I've taken on since the kids came to live with me."

"Is she all right?"

"She'll pull through, not much thanks to me."

The bitterness in his voice made her ask, "She tried to kill herself?"

"Closed the garage door, started her car and sat there with it running." His hand was clenched in a tight fist. "I never saw it coming."

Megan turned to face him, reading the pain and recrimination in his eyes. She laid her hand over his.

"Sam, it's not your fault."

"Part of me knows that. But there's a bigger part that wishes I could have guessed how deep her depression went—before she wound up in the hospital."

"But you said yourself she came to you only last week. How many sessions did you have with her?"

"Two. Today was supposed to be our third. When she didn't show up... I wondered... I had my secretary phone her. There wasn't any answer. Her teenage daughter found her barely in time."

"Sam." She took his hands in hers. "This has really hit you hard, hasn't it?"

He sighed heavily. "At the hospital, the daughter was half hysterical. The other two kids just sat there with fear written all over their faces. Their father had walked out on them. Got up one day, said, 'So long. Been nice knowing you' over breakfast and left."

"What happens to them now?"

Sam read the remembered pain in her eyes along with the compassion. She would undoubtedly have taken the children in, given the opportunity. He'd wanted to, as well, but he just couldn't take on any more responsibility. Besides, the rules and regulations hadn't allowed it.

"Social services will keep the kids until their mother is stabilized and able to go home," he said.

"Then you've done everything you can," Megan told him emphatically. She ached to see him hurting so, wanted to do something, anything, to take away this pain and lift his burden.

"I know," he said wearily. "But seeing her in that hospital bed, hearing her cry, knowing how scared her kids were..." His shoulders slumped. "All that reminded me how important it is to have someone to talk to. To hold you when you feel alone."

"Just hold," she said, remembering how much comfort he'd given her that first time he'd held her while she cried for the baby she'd lost.

"Just hold," he repeated. "No expectations, no pressure. I could really use that."

Megan didn't think twice. He needed consolation. Needed her. She opened her arms, and he gathered her close. How wonderful it felt to know she could give him comfort, take away some of the stress he was under.

He held her tightly, his arms strong, giving even as he took. She'd never felt so needed and cherished. Little by little, the tension seeped out of his muscles and he relaxed against her.

Sam inhaled the apple-blossom scent of her. The fragrance of heaven. He breathed it in again, holding her like a drowning man clings to a life preserver.

Tonight, at the hospital with his new patient and her frightened children, had made him face his limitations.

"Am I trying to do too much?" he asked, his chin lightly resting on Megan's head. "Am I shortchanging everyone in the process?"

She turned so she could look up at him. "Tonight when you came home, Becca raced out to see you and give you a hug. When she was at my house Sunday, the whole time she was painting she was telling me, 'Uncle Sam this' and 'Uncle Sam that.' She loves you."

"But Brian... He needs so much and I'm afraid—"

She pressed her fingers to his lips. "Don't be. You're there when he needs you. That smile he gave you when you came home—he was more than willing to lose an ounce or two of milk so he could smile at you."

"Yeah." He chuckled softly. "Before bedtime with him is the best part of the day."

"Having him fall asleep in your arms says a lot about love and trust. You've taken two children out of tragedy and made them happy. And you've helped me get over so much."

"I've done all that?" A small grin tugged at his mouth.

"Yes, but not all in one day, mind you."

He laughed. "That's right. Got to keep it in perspective, is that it?"

Her laughter was all he wanted. The sound surrounded him, filled every corner of his mind. He hugged her tightly, savored the feel of her arms around him as she hugged him back. This felt so good, so right and the feeling went all the way to the bone.

"Thank you, Megan," he said. "For the hug and the pep talk. You'd make a good psychologist."

She shook her head. "I'll stick with accounting, thank you very much. There aren't any surprises with numbers."

"I suppose not." Keeping one arm around her shoulders, he tucked her next to his side. "But there is something I've wondered about ever since you gave Becca that book—why does a woman with a strong creative side choose a career in accounting?"

"Because her very practical parents point out how difficult it is for most to make a living writing children's books."

"It can be done, though. Have you ever thought about it?"

"Abandoning my career as a C.P.A.?"

"Going after a new career," he amended.

She patted his hand. "I like where I'm at. My rhymes and paintings are just a hobby, and I'm happy with that."

"Happy. That's the key word." He was silent for a long moment.

"Still thinking about your patient?" she asked.

He breathed deeply. "Yeah. She never saw it coming—her husband leaving. He didn't even give her a chance. She's been trying to hold the children together and keep from falling apart herself. When the ER doctor revived her, all she could talk about was how overwhelmed she felt."

"You've been there, haven't you?" Megan asked sympathetically.

"Oh, yes."

"Then you'll be better able to help her through it."

"I guess that's what I'm afraid of—that I'll fail her and her kids. They lost their father and they're scared they've lost their mother, too."

"If she'll let you, you'll find a way to help her through it all."

"If she'll let me," he repeated thoughtfully. Then he nodded. "You're right. It has to be her decision." He sighed. "I don't know where all this self-pitying and these doubts have come from."

"From exhaustion." She wriggled out of his arms and stood up. "You need sleep. Brian was in a pretty good mood this evening, but..."

He groaned. "Don't remind me of how quickly that can change," he said, pulling himself up off the couch to walk her to the door.

On the porch she turned back to smile up at him. "By the way, thank you for the roses. I can't wait to pick them out. Did you know I'd been thinking about roses for the deck?"

He grinned. "Sunday, when you were rocking Brian and I was dishing up the Chinese food..."

"Yes," she prompted.

"There was a gardening magazine on the counter, open to an article on tending rosebushes. I took a chance that's what you were planning."

"Good instincts." To Sam's surprise, she stood on tiptoe and planted a quick kiss on his cheek. "Good night," she whispered, then rushed down the steps.

Sam watched her lithe figure until he saw the lights go on inside her house. As he went back inside and closed the door, he mused at what they'd shared tonight.

Except for his mother and sister, he'd never felt this close to a woman. In a sexual and yet a nonsexual way, as well. It had been wonderful to have Megan hold him, to hold her. This friendship with a woman he was attracted to was new to him.

But then his whole outlook on women and dating had been subtly changing since his sister's children had arrived on the scene. Spontaneity was good. Flexibility and dependability were better. A sense of humor was nice. Being able to handle Brian's teething was better yet.

Yes, he'd missed his former life. But precious few of his relationships had survived his life-style change. He'd been lamenting how easy he'd had it six months ago, but in truth, he wouldn't trade what he had with the kids.

And what he had with Megan?

He'd never found it this easy to talk to a woman, to allow himself to be vulnerable. Deep down he'd felt from the start that he could trust her with anything, even his deepest fears.

What he had with Megan? Something very special. But how far did he dare take things?

Chapter Nine

Megan carefully tamped down the last bit of dirt around
her newly planted azaleas and sat on her heels to examine
them. The small white blossoms with their pink-tipped edges
looked back at her with wide-eyed beauty. She'd planted
them exactly as the nursery owner had instructed. She only
hoped they would grow to be as lovely as the pictures he'd
shown her.

And the roses. She had to get the barrels yet and enough
soil to fill them, but she couldn't wait to show Sam the ones
she'd picked out. The blue and the coral and the yellow tea
roses were the most beautiful and fragrant roses she'd ever
seen and sniffed.

How lovely they would be alongside the three other rosebushes she'd picked out. How thoughtful Sam was to have
thought of them. He couldn't have sent her a gift that meant
more to her. He seemed to share her need to find the beauty
in life. Not merely understand it, but support that need as
well.

She was mentally going through the "what ifs," wishing for what couldn't be between her and Sam, when a noise made her turn toward the fence separating their yards. Becca stood there, holding the handle of her red wagon. There was a cardboard box squeezed tightly into it.

"Hi, Becca. What's in the box?"

The girl grinned slyly. "It's a present for you. I thought of it all by myself. Can I come in and give it to you?"

"Of course." Megan went to open the gate. "You didn't have to get me a present, sweetheart."

"But I want to," she said, wheeling the wagon to the deck steps.

Megan closed the gate, then followed Becca, stopping as she heard another sound. She could swear the noise came from inside the box. Sort of a squeak? Or had it been more of a yip? Very suspicious, she walked over to the deck.

"Open it!" Becca commanded excitedly.

As Megan reached for the flap, the box's contents let out a very definite yip. The box jumped. Something inside scratched to get outside, and Megan was very afraid she knew what that something was. She paused, already forming her objections to this particular "gift." But how could she refuse without hurting the child's feelings? Before she could come up with the right words, Becca had the flaps open.

The furry creature inside stood on his hind legs, front paws on the lip of the box. A ball of brown-and-white puppy fuzz, with long floppy ears, huge, soulful whiskey-colored eyes and a tail that wagged in a circle like the spring on a windup toy.

"Don't you just love him?" Becca sang out.

She lifted the pup out, holding him so his back paws dangled in the air. She raised him as high as her little arms could until Megan was forced to rescue the fellow.

"Him?" she asked.

Becca's grin widened to the max. "He's a boy."

"But..." Megan tried to get the puppy situated more securely in her arms. He had other ideas, though, such as swiping at her face with his wide, wet tongue.

"He loves you." Becca giggled. "Isn't it awesome? Now we both have puppies."

"Both?"

"Yeah. Isn't it awesome?" she asked again. "Uncle Sam said we could keep my puppy if it was okay with Emmaline, and it was. So I got one for you. He's the last one."

"Oh, Becca." Megan breathed deeply, gathering courage to say what had to be said. "Angel, this is very sweet of you—"

"I knew you would love Dusty."

"Dusty?"

"That's what me and Francie named him."

"Francie and I." Megan corrected her absently. What was she going to do about this unwelcome addition to her household given to her by a little girl with so much love and affection?

"Francie and I," Becca repeated hurriedly. "We called him that because Francie's mom said he liked to get under the couch and lay there like a dust ball."

Megan had to chuckle. At the sound of her soft laughter, the pup's tail wagged ferociously. He wriggled in her arms. Megan put him down. Nose to the grass, he explored his new surroundings with interest. He circled Becca, stopping to stand up with his front paws on her legs. When she ruffled the puppy's furry head, he barked his thanks, then ran off to explore some more.

Megan sat on the deck steps, then reached for Becca's hands. "Becca, a puppy is a big responsibility," she began.

"I know. It's lucky that you're a grown-up," the girl responded solemnly. "Uncle Sam and Emmaline have to help me with Amber."

"Amber?"

"That's what Francie's mom named my puppy, 'cause she has amber eyes."

"But, Becca," she said around a sigh. "Puppies are a lot like babies. They need someone to be around them most of the time. I work all day."

Becca frowned, then brightened. "I know. Amber and Dusty can play together while you're at work. Over here in your yard, maybe. That way Amber won't bother Emmaline so much when I'm at school in the mornings. And then when I get home, I'll get them water and play with them."

Becca was going to make it absolutely impossible for her to refuse, Megan realized. Becca would be crushed if she had to take the puppy back to Francie's and the pup had to go to the pound.

Megan had to admit the fellow was cute. Becca laid down on the grass and the pup scampered over her, barking, licking, tugging at her jeans, nipping at her shoelaces. Then he noticed Megan watching him. Eyes bright and mouth open in what could only be called a doggie smile, he dashed over to her, working his way under her hands until she petted him. In a very short time, he'd wormed his way onto her lap and was frantically trying to wash her face with his tongue.

Megan laughed at his antics and decided more laughter was just what she needed in her life. "Oh, why not?" she said to the pup. "You can stay."

Becca clapped her hands in delight. "I knew you would love him."

"What's not to love?" Megan said, catching his face in her hands for a quick caress. She put him on the grass, then glanced at her watch. "Guess I've got just enough time to hit the store and get him some things he'll need. Want to go with me?"

"Yeah! I'll go tell Uncle Sam and be right back!"

Megan had to catch Dusty to keep him from following Becca out the gate. "Ask your uncle if there's anything he needs while we're out."

In the end they all went to the pet store, Sam, Megan, the two kids and the two dogs. They put Brian in the shopping basket seat and the dogs in the back while they stocked up on puppy food, collars, leashes, bedding, dishes, treats and toys.

The last was very important, according to Becca who picked out two squeaky toys apiece for Dusty and Amber. Sam insisted on lots of chew-toys to keep the pups from going on search-and-destroy missions. Megan agreed.

They paid for everything and headed for the door. Megan stopped to pick up information pamphlets on vets, shots, worms, proper puppy nutrition and other important topics. Including obedience classes. The two pups romped in the back of the van on the way home, entertaining Brian and Becca.

"What have we gotten ourselves into?" Sam asked Megan very quietly.

"A lot of trouble and expense," she replied in the same quiet tone. "And some laughter and love."

He chuckled. "I swear I had no idea what Becca was going to do when she asked me to help her get her wagon out of the garage."

"Mmm. I thought seriously of killing you, or at least torturing you. But then Becca told me it was her idea."

Torture, Sam thought. Sounded kind of interesting. Providing it involved only the two of them and a deserted cabin in the mountains. God, he could imagine making love to her so vividly and in such mind-bending detail.

"It's a little hot in here, don't you think?" he asked, reaching for the fresh-air switch.

"Yes, it is." Megan had caught the heat in his eyes, and just the sight of it had created a heat inside her. The chemistry was there, the potential for danger and devastation. They'd managed to bank the fires, but somewhere in the back of her mind she wondered how long they would be able to keep the flames under control.

There was no future in wanting Sam, she told herself once Sam took her and Dusty home and she was settling the pup for the night. No future except heartache. Thinking of the hungry way in which he'd looked at her made her want to scream in frustration. It certainly didn't make falling asleep alone easy.

The moon was high in the sky and she'd been dreaming of Sam when something awakened her. She lay there with visions of their lovemaking still fresh in her mind and wondered what it would take to make her heart see reason. Then she heard Dusty.

He alternated his howling with a pitiful whine for attention, throwing in a few yips for good measure. Megan put the pillow over her head. This was the pup's first night alone in his new environment, she knew, but he'd have to get used to it.

A half hour of his cries was all she could stand. She got up and padded down the hall to the laundry room, a blanket over her arm and her travel alarm clock in her hand. Hopefully the warmth of the blanket and the ticking of the clock would settle him down.

His barks changed from pitiful to playful when she opened the door. He danced around her ankles in delight, yipping and yapping excitedly. She piled the blanket on the pad in his wicker bed and put the clock on the floor beside it. He sniffed both, then tried to follow Megan out of the room.

Three times she picked him up and set him on the blanket and three times he chased after her, beating her to the door. In desperation, she let him outside in case a full bladder might be what was keeping him awake. As she stood on the deck, she saw the kitchen lights go on in Sam's house.

Remembering Brian's earache from a few nights ago, she decided to phone Sam and see if he needed help. She got the cordless phone and dialed his number.

"Is Brian all right?" she asked when he answered, his voice definitely gruff.

"Yes. He's sleeping like a baby. No pun intended."

"Then let me guess," she said, hearing the frustration behind his words. "It's Amber."

He growled. "I should have my head examined for agreeing to take the mongrel. What the hell ever possessed me to say yes to this deal?"

"A little girl with big blue eyes and a lower lip that pouts out just enough to make it impossible to say no."

He laughed at that, then sighed. "Dusty keeping you up, too?"

"Yup. I thought letting him out would help, but I think he's not going to like the idea of sleeping alone any more after he does his chores than he did before."

"Well, I'm out of ideas for getting this one to quiet down and go to sleep, and about out of patience, too. This is the first night in days that one or the other of the kids hasn't been up and instead of sleeping, I'm ... I'm ... Bad dog," he said. "No, no, no."

Megan listened, smiling as he continued to scold the dog.

"I give up," he finally said to her. "I spent a small fortune on toys for this mutt, and all she wants to do is chew the wicker on her bed."

"I have an idea," Megan said, hearing that he was at his wit's end and in need of a break from the last few day's stress. Instant fatherhood and all the accompanying problems was taking its toll on him. "Why don't I get Amber and she and Dusty can keep each other company over here?"

She could tell he was considering the idea, seriously, but then his conscience got the better of him. "I couldn't take advantage of you like that. Could I?"

"It's worth a try," she persisted. "They miss each other and they might actually sleep if they have someone familiar to cuddle down with."

Bad choice of words, she decided as her mind conjured up an image of her cuddling down with Sam. A much too vivid image, complete with the peace, contentment and excitement that would come with it.

"Well . . ." Sam said slowly.

Megan marveled that even in the throes of exhaustion, he would be considerate of her needs. "Put her leash on her and I'll come and get her. Let's try it before we lose any more sleep."

"Yeah, I can't afford to lose much more." He chuckled wryly. "It's a deal, providing you agree to have dinner with me Saturday night. I should be able to line up a sitter between now and then."

Megan hesitated. Dinner with him was another step in a dangerous direction.

"I won't take no for an answer," he said before she could formulate her protest. "I'll have Amber ready in sixty seconds flat."

The phone line went dead. With a sigh, Megan switched off her phone and donned her robe and slippers. Amber was doing hyperactive circles around Sam, tangling him in her leash as he tried to get her down the steps. Megan heard a curse or two and a lot of grumbling as he waited for her.

But it wasn't the pup that held her attention. In the moonlight she saw Sam was clad in pajama bottoms and nothing more. Her steps hesitated. Seeing him this way seemed so intimate. Her breath caught as all her longings hit her full force. As it did each time she was near him, her need for him ran out of control.

She wanted to rush into his arms, to give herself up to the passion she knew would be there, waiting for her. Her heart was determined to ignore the pain that would come when Sam found a woman to bear his children.

Why did her heart always lead her in the wrong direction?

She breathed deeply and walked up to the bottom porch step. Sam studied her silently for a long moment. She could read his desire there on his face and felt her pulse pick up its pace.

"I hope you know what you're doing," he told her, finally breaking the silence.

"So do I. Good night, Sam."

She left, not trusting herself to stay another minute in his company. He looked so tempting, his hair tousled, a scowl of frustration on his handsome face. She'd wanted to take him in her arms, to kiss him and make everything better. But in the middle of the night, with the moonlight casting its spell, she knew exactly where that would lead.

Sam watched Megan walk back to her house, experiencing a strong desire to go with her. But he couldn't do that. It was all he could manage to keep his hands to himself as it was.

To be in the same room with her... to lie next to her, loving and talking into the night... He'd sell his soul for a night of passion with her. Bargain with the devil for just one more chance to kiss her again. With a sigh, he went back inside,

lving himself up to thoughts of making love to her as he
cifted into sleep.

Thursday evening Sam took Megan and the kids to
lcDonalds, then out to pick up the oak kitchen set and end
ables she'd ordered. On the trip back to her house, Megan
ied not to yawn, at least not so Sam could notice.

The two pups liked to play together at night. The first
ight the pair had romped in the laundry room into the wee
ours before finally settling down. Last night Megan had
ollected Amber once Sam had Brian and Becca tucked in
ed, hoping some playtime in the backyard before bed
ould tire the dogs out before she put them in the laundry
oom. They'd slept—until around two when Dusty had
oused Amber and tried teaching her to howl at the moon.

In between the half-dozen scoldings Megan had given the
uppies, she'd looked over at Sam's house and had been
appy to note the lights were out. He was finally catching up
n missed sleep. He appeared more refreshed tonight. His
ves were less weary and his smile came often. Megan took
reat pleasure in knowing she'd had a hand in that.

She was caring too much. Allowing her emotions to get
volved much too deeply. But she couldn't summon the
illpower to stop herself.

"I hope Dusty and Amber didn't get through the fence,"
ecca said as Sam backed the van up Megan's driveway.

"As fat as those two have gotten," Sam remarked dryly,
there's no place big enough for them to squeeze through."

Megan smiled. Becca and Brian's favorite pastimes had
en to overfeed the puppies, and the two furballs were only
o happy to accept each and every treat.

"Can me and Bri play with Amber and Dusty while you
ke the tables in?" Becca asked, unbuckling her seat belt
e second Sam shut off the engine.

"Sure," Megan said, lifting Brian out of his car seat. "Let's go in through the house, though. That way we won't have to worry about them running out the gate."

Becca raced up to the front door. Once Megan had it opened, the girl tore through the living room and kitchen and out the back door.

"Dusty," Becca said, staring down at him, "where'd you get that?"

Megan looked down to see the pup holding a leafy branch in his mouth, then noticed the small blooms. Her mouth opened on a strangled gasp as she recognized the branch he dropped at her feet.

Finally she found her voice. "Bad dog." He lowered his head a notch, but other than that, he didn't seem overly concerned with Megan's anger. "Becca, watch your brother, would you, please?"

She sat Brian down and snatched up the azalea bush. It was bruised and chewed beyond recovery. With a growl and a sigh, Megan carried the plant inside, sadly laid it to rest in the trash can, then went to give Sam a hand. He'd already carried in the end tables and was unloading the kitchen chairs and table base.

He studied her expression for a long moment, then asked, "Is something wrong?"

"Dusty. He ate one of my azaleas."

"He *ate* a plant?"

She nodded. "Dug it up or pulled it up. I'm not sure which. I couldn't bear to look." She reached for her end of the tabletop and froze. Her mouth opened on a small gasp. "What if it's poisonous?"

Sam considered this. "Some houseplants are, I know. Didn't you get the names of a couple of vets from the pet store?"

"Yes. One of them had an emergency number, too. Let's carry this in and then I'll call." She sighed. "To think the little mutt was named because he liked to hide under furniture," she muttered, picking up her end of the tabletop. "He's sure done an about-face."

Sam chuckled. "Maybe he's the kind who doesn't shine in a crowd."

"Spoken like a true psychiatrist. Are you branching out into the animal kingdom now, Doctor?"

"Bite your tongue, woman. I've got as much as I can handle with the humans. But I would like to point out that *my* pup seems to be innocent of any crimes."

"Go ahead and gloat," she said as they eased the top into the kitchen and set it to rest against the cabinets. "Then take a look at Dusty's wicker bed." She opened the laundry room door. Pieces of wicker and bedding were trailed over most of the floor.

"Ah, but can you prove it was Amber?"

"My dog was lying on the blanket in the corner, sleeping. Yours was in the middle of the mess with pieces of wicker still in her mouth. And if that isn't close enough to a smoking gun, I clearly recall you scolding her for doing the same thing to her own bed."

He grinned sheepishly. "Why did we ever agree to take in these troublesome creatures?"

"Becca got to us in a moment of weakness. And speaking of your niece…" She turned to glance out the back door. "Sam, look."

He put down his screwdriver and went to peer over her shoulder. Becca and Brian were in the grass with the puppies. Becca appeared to be having a very serious conversation with Dusty. Amber was running circles around Brian. The more he laughed, the harder the dog ran.

"A photo opportunity," Sam said from his place behind her, close enough he could inhale the fresh scent of her shampoo.

"Kinda makes it worth the trouble," she said, reaching for the phone and punching out the emergency number for the vet.

"Almost."

Because he needed to touch her, he laid a hand on her shoulder. He stood there, wishing he had the right to take her in his arms, to do so much more. He'd never felt closer to another woman and on every level—physical, emotional, sexual. That last was causing him some major problems, trying to shut off needs he'd never had trouble controlling with anyone else.

"Well, the vet says it won't kill him," she said around a relieved sigh as she hung up the phone. "But it might make him sick, depending on how much got into his system."

"Serves the little bugger right," Sam said with only a slight trace of sympathy for the pup.

Megan looked up at him. "He didn't know any better, Sam. I should have anticipated his getting into this kind of mischief."

"Okay, so now we invest in fences around the garden, as well as a new bed for Dusty." He growled softly. "And then we try to find some way to keep Amber from supplementing her daily fiber intake with wicker."

Smiling, Megan leaned back just a little. It felt good to be this close to him, to have at least this tiny bit of contact. For one brief moment, she wouldn't think of all the reasons against it.

Too soon Becca spotted them watching her and ran up to the deck. "Dusty's really sorry, Megan," she said very solemnly.

"Then he's forgiven."

"You're being too easy on him," Sam said in a voice only Megan could hear. "Tell her he's still in the doghouse."

She chose to ignore the remark. "I'll bring everyone inside, then I can help you set the top on the table base."

Reluctantly, Sam let her go—something that was becoming harder to do each time he had to do it. He wanted her so badly, but she wasn't the type for a casual fling. Neither was he. Not since... What? he asked himself as he carried in the table base. Not since the kids came, or not since Megan?

Interesting question, indeed. With an elusive answer. Was he looking at Megan in terms of something lasting? She was so good with his children and the two pups. He couldn't get enough of the way she looked and the way she smelled, the sound of her laughter, the sight of her smile. Her ready wit and humor had gotten him through quite a few rough times.

He had a lot to think about as he finished setting up her table, then gathered the kids, took them home and got them into bed. He wasn't the only one who had Megan on his mind, either. Becca took forever to wind down, chattering on about how good Megan was to forgive Dusty and not throw Amber out on her ear for destroying the wicker bed.

Megan. He could close his eyes and picture her holding Brian, laughing with Becca, sharing a private smile with him. Then there was that attraction and passion between them. He wanted her and when he looked at her, he often read an answering need in the depths of her soft brown eyes.

He understood she was desperately trying to keep some perspective in their friendship and knew that he should be doing the same. But he couldn't seem to get his need for her under control.

He was very definitely glad he'd exchanged Amber's nighttime crying for dinner on Saturday. Dinner *and* dancing, he decided. He wouldn't tell Megan until it was too late for her to be nervous and perhaps refuse him.

Holding a woman close was perfectly legal on the dance floor. No way was he going to let her talk him out of it.

Chapter Ten

With uncharacteristic nervousness, Sam watched Megan cut into her filet mignon and take a bite. Only when she pronounced it a fantastic cut of steak, perfectly prepared, did he relax. He wanted everything about this evening to be special—unforgettable. Tonight, seeing her smile was the most important thing in his life.

"How's your prime rib?" she asked, making him realize he'd been staring too long. But he couldn't seem to take his eyes off her tonight.

"Great. It's great."

"I like the cattle-baron atmosphere here," she said.

He smiled, feeling pleased. "This is the premier steak house in Kansas City."

He was just grateful the place hadn't changed in the months since he'd been here last. But sitting across from Megan, the stress of the past six months faded into nothing.

"So was Becca okay with your leaving her tonight?" she asked.

"Better than usual, but I doubt she'll ever be entirely comfortable with it."

"That's understandable. Maybe having the dogs there will keep her mind occupied and she won't worry so much."

Sam smiled wryly. "She intends to give Dusty a serious talking to about his digging in your garden."

Megan laughed. "I told her puppies will be puppies, but she takes her responsibility in this very seriously."

"Sometimes I worry she's too responsible. That maybe circumstances have made her grow up too fast."

"Oh, I think there's still plenty of the little girl in her," Megan offered. "But I suppose it's natural to worry."

"I think there's a rule somewhere that the capacity for excessive and needless worry is a prerequisite for parenthood."

"That and a sense of humor."

"And someone to talk to. Someone special." His smile warmed.

Megan felt that warmth reach out to her, tempting, testing her will—what little of it she had around this man. More and more she found herself wondering what it would be like to surrender to her own passion. The heat in his eyes made her uncomfortable—in a sexually expectant way.

"How's your hospital patient?" she asked in an effort to redirect her wayward thoughts.

"Better." He set his fork down and reached for his glass of scotch. "She's worried about her children, thinking about someone outside herself. It's a start." He looked into Megan's eyes. "It's not something I normally do, but I've talked to her about how difficult sudden parenthood is for me to deal with, and that I couldn't have handled Brian's teething half as well without a friend. Without you."

"Me?" Those expressive eyes of hers widened. "I didn't do anything."

"You were there and you listened."

"Yes, but anyone—"

"Not anyone," he insisted. "Most of my friends, and occasionally even my partners, would see me coming and run in the other direction for fear of being treated to an account of the latest trauma." He laid his hand over hers on the white tablecloth. "I want you to know how much I value our friendship and how glad I am that you came into my life, Megan McAllister."

"Sam . . . I . . . You're a very good friend . . ."

He sighed inwardly at the emphasis she put on that last word. She was struggling to keep their relationship within the nice, safe boundaries they'd drawn up. Struggling no harder than he. But Sam longed to live dangerously, to just this once go with his feelings and not ponder through the possible aftermath. However, he wouldn't for the world risk hurting Megan.

He turned her hand in his when she would have pulled away. "Let's go dancing."

Megan blinked. "Dancing?"

The word held so much promise and possibilities. So much danger. How could he suggest it? How could her pulse beat this fast and furious in anticipation? How could she resist the lure of her own longings? Because she couldn't find it in her heart to deny him anything.

"But Becca . . ." she said, hoping the thought of his niece would change his mind.

"I told her I wouldn't be home until very late. And I told Jill's parents not to expect her home before midnight."

That made mincemeat of any objection Megan could voice, except the one she couldn't find the willpower to put into words. There was an air of unreality to the evening, as if there were no obstacles to letting their feelings, their needs and desires, run wild.

She knew trouble when it grinned back at her with laughing blue eyes and devastatingly deep dimples. But for tonight, for the warmth and promise in Sam's smile, she would put the future on hold.

"All right," she said slowly. "Dancing."

The pleasure her answer gave him lit the depths of his eyes. His smile was both boyishly excited and all-male at the same time. They finished their meal, he signaled the waitress for the check, then before Megan knew it, he was helping her into the passenger seat of his sports car.

He drove to a club on the Plaza. Before Megan could think of all the reasons against it, she found herself on the dance floor and in his arms. The music swirled around her, slow and sensual. Her heart matched its beat to the pulsating rhythm, matching Sam's heartbeat. She could feel it strong and steady where he held her hand to his chest.

How she'd craved the feel of his arms around her, holding her in his tight embrace. There was the contentment and the excitement of the attraction between them. And the fervent longing to explore every aspect of that chemistry. She couldn't allow that, but she couldn't change the course of her need.

Sam was alone with her. In a room crowded with couples, there was only the two of them and the sensual haze of the music. Oh, but this felt so very right, having her pressed against him, her head against his shoulder, her slender body in his arms, her soft curves melded to the length of him.

He wanted her like never before, but he also wanted this moment to last. As much as he longed to kiss her, to ignite the embers of passion that smoldered in the depths of her eyes, he knew he wouldn't give in. He would hold his need in check. If he told her of it, if he so much as hinted at how much he ached for her, she would pull away.

He wasn't being wise, he knew, playing with fire this way. But the scent of her hair, of her creamy skin, was driving him to distraction. Out of his mind. Past the power of rational thought.

Megan sighed softly as the musicians played another slow and dreamy tune. It was a conspiracy, all the elements and forces at work to make her weak. She knew Sam held her much too close, breasts to chest, thigh to thigh, but she couldn't make herself object. Reason was overruled, subdued.

She wanted this moment to go on forever. She'd long ago given up her childish belief in happily-ever-after endings, but looking up into Sam's eyes, she could almost believe in love again.

Almost. Need. Lust. Those she could understand. They were down-to-earth, nitty-gritty emotions. Love was in a totally different class. For her love was fickle. Just when she thought she'd found it, when she was sure it would last this time, it disappeared like a wisp of smoke.

But here and now, these feelings were very real. She leaned into Sam as he moved her to the soft strains of the acoustic guitar. She had no idea how long they danced or the length of time they sat at an intimate table tucked in a corner, sipping iced cappuccino and talking. She only knew that there was nowhere else she wanted to be than here with Sam.

It was nearly two o'clock when he parked in his driveway and walked Megan back to her house.

"I hope Becca's not upset," she said as they stood on her small porch. She suddenly felt awkward and unsure. She truly wanted Sam to kiss her good-night. Had been wanting him to kiss her all night. Now that the moment was here, though, reason began to tentatively assert itself.

"She's apt to be more upset that we didn't bring her ice cream," Sam said. "But since the only light on in the house is the one in the TV room, I'd bet she's asleep and has been for a long while."

"Your keen observation wouldn't have anything to do with the quick telephone call you made to Jill when you went to the men's room, would it?"

Sam chuckled. "Caught."

He jammed his hands into his pockets. If he didn't, he would certainly take Megan in his arms again. Without the spell of music and dim candlelight, that didn't seem like a good idea.

They'd reached a special and all-too-fragile point in their relationship, he sensed, and he was afraid to do anything to destroy that. She'd let him hold her on the dance floor. He'd felt her desire answering his own need, and now he wanted only to make love to her, but he couldn't rush things now. They both needed time to see where these feelings were leading. He leaned close to her and lightly brushed his mouth over her cheek.

"Tomorrow," he said softly, bending close enough that she could feel his breath fan her face. "We're going to the zoo."

Megan was inside the house and Sam was gone before she could decide whether she was already in over her head where her feelings for Sam were concerned.

It was going to hurt, Megan decided as they trooped through the tropical forest the next afternoon. Really tear her apart when Sam met someone else to share his life. She'd done what she'd vowed never to do again. She'd led with her heart.

And now she realized how very much she cared for Sam and his small family. The way Brian begged for her to hold him. The way Becca hung on her every word. The way Sam smiled at her, making her feel giddy and weak-kneed.

What was she going to do about all this? There was no going back and no wisdom in going ahead. She knew that and yet she couldn't change her feelings.

Holding Brian as he pointed at the rare birds and tried to mimic their squeaks and squawks, Megan suddenly realized why she'd never told Sam about her hysterectomy. By keeping that last bit of her sorrow to herself, she'd hoped to keep a fraction of emotional distance between them. She hadn't succeeded.

She also realized she'd withheld the information for another totally selfish reason. She wanted to hold onto him a little longer. Once he knew the truth, he would leave her, and she couldn't bear that.

"This little guy's got to be getting heavy," Sam said, fondly chucking Brian under the chin. "Come on, kiddo. Wanna go for a ride?"

Brian squirmed out of her grasp and into his uncle's. Once Sam settled the boy on his shoulders, Brian immediately ruffled Sam's hair.

"You little stinker," Sam scolded around a laugh.

Becca giggled. "I taught him to do that."

"And you're real proud of yourself." Grinning, Sam finger-combed his hair.

Watching him smile down at her, it hit Megan—she loved him. Completely. Stupidly.

Sam saw all the color drain from Megan's face. It happened so suddenly, it startled him.

"Megan," he gasped. "Are you all right?"

She didn't answer. Just stared at him, or more accurately, through him. Her gaze was unfocused. He took her arm and led her to the stone bench nearby.

"Megan," he said again.

She blinked then, swallowed hard and inhaled deeply. A tiny bit of color returned to her delicate cheeks.

"I'm okay," she said in a near whisper.

Sam remained unconvinced.

"Really." The smile she gave him was very shaky, though. "The humidity in here got to me. That's all."

"You're probably exhausted, too," he said, still watching her closely. "I kept you up most of the night, then I dragged you to the zoo—"

Becca had run a little ahead on the asphalt path through the lush greenery and now returned to announce, "I'm hungry."

"Food is a good idea," Megan agreed, though it was the last thing she wanted. "It is past lunchtime."

Hearing her, Brian kicked his feet and thumped Sam on the head.

"Lunch is the magic word as far as this kid's concerned. He wants lunch and he wants it now." Sam reached into the bag in the back of the stroller, found two boxes of raisins and gave one to each of the kids. He settled Brian in the stroller, then extracted another raisin box from the diaper bag and gave it to Megan, insisting she munch on that as they looked for one of the food stands.

"Well," he said as he studied the menu of the first one they found, "it appears our choices are greasy hamburgers and fries or greasy hot dogs and fries."

"Hamburger," Becca exclaimed.

Brian babbled his agreement.

Sam cast Megan a quick glance. "Four burgers?"

She nodded, then herded the two children to one of the tables while Sam put in their order.

It was one of those unusually warm and sunny spring afternoons and the recently renovated zoo had drawn a fair crowd. She and Sam and the two children looked much like the other families. With one important distinction. They weren't a family.

No amount of wishing could make it so. Her place in this picture was temporary. One day someone else would take her place—another woman. One who would help Sam fill the picture with more eager, smiling faces.

When he'd gaze at this woman, his eyes would fill with desire as they did now when he looked at Megan. He would smile at someone else with that warm and wonderfully entrancing smile. He would take that special someone else and hold her in his arms, kiss her, make love—

"It's too bad we couldn't bring Amber and Dusty with us," Becca said in a chirp, her short legs swinging in the air under the picnic-table bench. "They could make some new animal friends."

"No way," Sam told her as he set the food on the table. "Those two mongrels get into enough trouble by themselves. I will not have them inviting their animal friends over to add to the problems."

Becca looked crestfallen at his harsh tone.

"Sam, they're just pups," Megan said, breaking a french fry in half and blowing to cool it before she handed it to Brian.

"Just pups my a—my foot," he said, unwrapping Becca's hamburger. "Those two are a pair of four-footed demolition experts. Nothing in the house or the yard is safe from them."

"They chewed up my book bag," Becca said.

"You know that deep hole Dusty dug in your garden?" he asked Megan. "Well, I'm sure he and Amber were plotting to bury the bag's remains there."

Megan tried unsuccessfully to contain a grin. "They figured they couldn't be convicted without a body—or in this case a dead book bag—as evidence, huh?"

"Right." Sam bit into a french fry and chewed furiously. "You can laugh if you want, but think about this. With those two around, you'll be lucky if you get so much as one string bean in the way of produce from that garden. And now Becca has to go to school tomorrow and tell her teacher the dog ate her homework. Miss Lopez will laugh her out of school."

Becca frowned over at him. "We don't have homework in kindergarten. Don't you remember? It was a picture I made of Amber and Dusty. I was going to show it to Miss Lopez."

"I'm sure the FBI would have liked to have that picture to hang on the post office walls. Numbers one and two on the Ten Least Wanted List."

Megan's laughter escaped. She knew Sam well enough to recognize his grumbling was really good-natured. He was venting. However, he could only endure so much frustration before something had to give.

"I think perhaps it's time to register those two for school," she suggested.

"Yeah! A military boarding school for canine juvenile delinquents." He sipped his soft drink as he mulled over the idea, then he sighed. "It would never work. The pair of them would be expelled before the end of the first week."

"Very funny," Megan said, dipping a fry into the mound of ketchup he'd put on her open hamburger wrapper. "I was thinking of obedience school. The dog and the owner go to one class a week and—"

"The dog *and* the owner?" he demanded aghast.

"You learn how to give specific commands, and the dog learns how to obey."

"Commands? Like run away and never come back?"

Becca gasped and choked on her drink. Megan thumped her back until her coughs subsided.

"Tell her you were joking, Sam," Megan insisted, giving him a quelling stare.

"I *was* kidding, sweetheart," he said, gently tugging one of her curls.

"But you're really mad at Amber for chewing a hole in my book bag?"

"Not really," he acknowledged. "Amber is little, like Brian is little. You know how we have to be careful that he doesn't get into things that might hurt him?"

She nodded. "He puts *everything* in his mouth."

"That's exactly what puppies do."

"So maybe you need to find another place to leave your book bag," Megan offered. "And tomorrow morning I'll call and set up obedience classes."

Becca's smile was brilliant. "Yea! Can I go with them, too?"

Sam laughed. "Sounds like a plan to me."

And a damn good plan at that, he thought with pleasure. This would guarantee that he would have a chance to be with Megan at least once a week for the classes. Then there would be practice sessions, wouldn't there? As dense as those two pups were, their training was bound to be long and involved. Which meant there could be many evenings and weekends spent with Megan.

She was quieter, pensive, Sam noted as they continued on their tour of the zoo. He was glad to be the first to show her some of the sites of Kansas City, the first to see her eyes light up as she took it all in.

Gradually Megan's animation and enthusiasm returned. Sam was grateful for that even as he wondered what had caused her to pale back there in the tropical forest. Had she perhaps been feeling some of the same emotions that were assailing him? Did she share the awareness that what they were feeling for each other was deeper than friendship?

He hoped so. Man, he hoped so. The more he was with her, the more he realized that what he felt for her was new and different from anything he'd experienced before. Like shooting the rapids without a raft or a life jacket. It was some ride, and he found it even more exciting to think Megan might be taking the wild ride with him.

He held onto that thought as they walked the last stretch of the zoo, packed the exhausted kids into the van, drove to a restaurant for dinner, then headed for home.

All in all it had been a wonderful day, he thought as he shut off the van's engine. He lifted a truly tired Becca out while Megan carefully maneuvered a dead-to-the-world Brian out of his car seat. Seeing the baby cuddle down against her breast, Sam felt a set of incredibly strong longings—to make love to her, to see her carrying his child, their child.

In a daze he followed her up the porch steps, then unlocked the door. Inside he set Becca on the couch.

"Do you want me to take him?" he asked, turning to Megan, noting the faint blush today's sunshine had put on her lovely face.

She shook her head. "I think I can manage. Maybe it would be better if I didn't wake him up by trying to wrestle him into his pajamas, though."

"Great idea." He watched her walk down the hall, savoring the gentle sway of her hips, the way she looked holding the sleeping infant.

"The answering machine is blinking," Becca said around a yawn.

Sam reached over to push the Replay button, tugging Becca's sneakers off as the tape rewound and then played back the messages.

"Sam, it's Paul Fletcher."

His attorney? Working on the weekend?

"I know it's Sunday, but I have news that you've been waiting for. I guess it actually came in on Thursday, but I was in Joplin and I just found these papers in the stack of stuff Amanda piled on my desk. I came in today to start sorting through some of this—"

Paul's words were drowned out by the machine's shrill beep. There were a couple more beeps, then Paul's voice again.

"Guess I'm getting long-winded in my old age," he said, chuckling. "The point of all this is that the adoption papers are here on my desk and you are now legally a dad. Congratulations, Papa. You can come by my office tomorrow and deliver my cigar."

Sam's heart tripped all over itself. He glanced up at Becca, who now watched him with a frown of uncertainty.

"Did the judge say it was okay for you to 'dopt me and Brian?" she asked in a small voice.

"Yes, he did." Sam took her tiny hands in his and gazed into her wide blue eyes. "How do you feel about it?"

"Happy."

Sam detected a hint of hesitancy, though. "But?" he prompted gently.

She breathed deeply. "What about my real daddy? And my mommy?"

"What about them?" Sam wanted to know. He needed her to voice her fears so there would be no misunderstanding between them.

"Will they be mad because Daddy can't be my real daddy anymore?"

This adjusting to the new status quo in their lives wasn't easy for any of them, especially for Becca. There was so much she didn't understand, hard as she tried. He sat beside her on the couch and lifted her onto his lap.

"Your daddy and mommy will always be your daddy and mommy. As long as you live. No judge will change that. Ever," he stressed. "But they can't be here to talk to us, or to take care of you and Brian."

"Because they had to go to heaven?"

"Right," Sam replied patiently. They'd covered much of this ground before, but he would go over it again and again, as many times as it took to make her comfortable with the situation. "So they asked me to take care of you."

"And you have to 'dopt us because they aren't here?"

"And because I want to. Daddy number two—you could think of me that way. I have to be your legal dad so I can get you into schools and take you to the doctor and all those things Mommies and Daddies have to do to take care of their children."

She was quiet for what seemed an eternity to Sam, her curly blond head resting against his chest. Finally Sam couldn't stand the silence any longer.

"Becca," he said very softly. The words would be the hardest he would ever have to say, he was sure, but they had to be said. "You don't have to call me Daddy if it makes you sad."

She looked up at him, her little eyes full of tears. "I miss my daddy," she said. "Real bad. But if I can't have him and Mommy, I want you." She threw her arms around his neck, hugging him tightly. Her mouth close to his ear, she said, "I love you. Daddy."

So much unconditional love and blind trust, Sam thought, returning her fierce embrace. He only hoped he could live up to all her expectations—now and forever.

"I love you, too, angel." He could barely speak around the lump in his throat.

After a minute Becca pulled away to gaze at him. This beautiful child who was now his daughter smiled at him,

hen rested her forehead on his and tried to look into his
yes. Arms still around his neck, she giggled.

"Daddy," she said and giggled again.

"Daughter." Sam laughed softly, knowing in his heart
hat everything would be fine.

"Now all we need to be a real family is a mommy."

The two of them turned their heads as they heard Megan
oming down the hallway.

"I know," Becca said excitedly as soon as she caught a
limpse of Megan. "Megan can be our mommy."

FAMILY IS THE BOSS...

Chapter Eleven

That was exactly what he wanted, Sam realized. Megan te be by his side, to share the little upsets and big joys, to love.

"What was that?" she asked with a smile for Becca.

The girl jumped down from Sam's lap and dashed over to Megan. "Uncle Sam is my daddy now. We want you to be my mommy."

Yes, Sam's heart shouted. With Megan, his life would be complete at last. She was what he'd been missing for so long now.

Then he recognized the expression in her eyes. The eyes of the woman he loved. Panic. He felt more than a touch of that himself. This was a lifetime step he was contemplating Love had caught him when he wasn't looking, and he was still reeling from the surprise.

Becca threw her arms around Megan's waist. "I love you."

Megan's heart was stammering painfully. That's what Becca and Sam had been discussing when she'd walked in

She hadn't heard. Oh, God, what had she done? How had she let things go this far, get this far out of hand?

But she knew the answer to that. Being with Sam and his children had made her laugh. With them she'd felt cherished. They'd renewed her joy in living. She felt whole and happy. Now her selfishness in hanging onto Sam and Becca and Brian—even while she'd known she shouldn't—would haunt her forever.

"Oh, Becca" was all she could say. What could she tell the little girl? How could she made her understand? What words could she use to spare her pain?

"Come on, sweetheart. Bedtime," Sam said, coming up to the child.

Megan glanced up at him, into those beautiful, trusting eyes of his, and died a little inside.

"I want Megan—" Becca protested.

"Not tonight," Sam told her. "Megan and I have to have a grown-up talk."

As the two walked down the hall, Megan wrapped her arms around herself. The pain was intense. It ripped through her.

And this was just the beginning. She would have to tell Sam about the hysterectomy. Then she would have to let him go. It would hurt him. And Becca. Megan knew she would have all the lonely nights and days to come to remember the pain she'd caused them all. Because she knew now that Sam loved her. She'd seen it in his eyes.

"Well, she's down," Sam said, coming back into the room. "But I can't guarantee for how long. She's pretty excited."

Megan felt the first tear trail down her cheek. "Sam," she whispered around the tightness in her throat. "I'm sorry. So very sorry."

Sam froze. He'd been about to take her in his arms, to kiss her. Between kisses he'd planned to tell her how much he loved her. But she was crying.

Something was wrong with this picture. Sam had to know what, yet he desperately wished they could go back to the way things had been before Becca blurted out her suggestion that Megan be her mother.

"What is it, Megan?" He braced, waiting, hoping, fearing.

"I never meant for things to go this far." Megan needed him to understand. Looking into his eyes, she knew what she was about to do to him. She knew what it felt like to have someone you loved and trusted cut your heart out and trample it to death.

"If you're afraid we're rushing things..." But Sam was certain there was more to her tears than their relationship moving too fast for her.

"I should have told you before," she said, sniffing.

"Then tell me now," he said softly. *Please, let it be something we can work out.*

"When Joey... After he was born..."

She bit her lower lip so hard it was a wonder she didn't draw blood. Sam wanted to take her into his arms, hold her and promise to make everything all right. But he wasn't sure it was a promise she would let him keep. So he waited and prayed like never before.

"Afterward..." She breathed deeply and straightened as if preparing for battle.

Sam didn't want to fight her. He only wanted to love her the rest of his life.

"The bleeding didn't stop." She finally got out the words. Her tears flowed more heavily now. "The doctor said the placenta separated prematurely. That was why he was born too early. Then the bleeding... They tried everything, but it wouldn't stop. Finally they had to operate. Do a... hysterectomy.''

Now it all made sense, Sam thought. The pain in her eyes the first time she saw Becca. The way seeing Brian had resurrected all her grief. The way she looked at the boy the first time she held him in her arms.

But what was even clearer was that she hadn't trusted Sam enough to tell him. He'd confided so much in her—everything. And she'd held back.

"Why are you telling me this now?" he demanded, surprised at the coldness of his own voice.

He was going to hate her, Megan realized. She heard the beginnings of it in his tone and she couldn't blame him.

"Because of what Becca said—"

"That's not what I meant. You said you should have told me before. Why didn't you?"

"That day I gave Becca and her friend painting lessons, she said you promised her brothers and sisters. I just couldn't tell you."

A muscle in his jaw worked. "Why? You'd told me everything else. Or have you?"

"There's nothing else." Megan drew in a ragged breath. Arms still wrapped around her middle, she stared at the carpet. She couldn't stand seeing the hurt and anger in Sam's eyes. "I'm so sorry."

"Sorry?" Sam bit out the words. She'd withheld the most important part of what she'd gone through. Why hadn't she told him she couldn't have children?

"Sorry," he said again. "I'm sure that's what your husband said before he walked out the door. And what the doctors said when they had to operate and when they couldn't save your son. How much good did it do you for them to say they were sorry?"

He didn't raise his voice. Maybe if he raged at her, she could take refuge in returning his fury. But all she could hear was the hurt, and she would carry that with her always. He was right. Sorry hadn't eased any of her pain and it wouldn't take away his.

She raised her chin, ready to face the consequences of her selfish actions. "You're right. There's nothing I can say to justify not telling you."

He shoved his hands into his pockets, but not before Megan saw his white-knuckled fists. "You didn't trust me. I thought I meant something to you, that we meant something to each other, but I guess I was wrong."

She heard the ice in his tone. Saw it in his eyes. There was nothing left. If begging would have made a difference, she would have swallowed her pride and pleaded with him to forgive her. But nothing would change the fact that she couldn't give him the children he wanted.

She walked to the door, turning back for one last, hopeful second. Those eyes that had gazed at her with such warmth now glared at her with cold anger. She pulled the door closed behind her.

Sam wanted to smash something. How could Megan have led him on? Let him believe she cared for him and the kids?

As soon as those thoughts took shape, though, he had to acknowledge that she *had* cared. If she hadn't, she would have laughed in his face. Instead she'd cried. The tears had been genuine, and through his own fury, he hurt as much for her as he did for himself.

And for Becca.

Damn! Give it awhile and Brian wouldn't even remember Megan's brief part in his life. But Becca . . . She was going to remember and hurt. She was still trying to come to terms with her parents leaving her. How the hell could he explain that Megan couldn't be that missing part of their lives no matter how badly Becca wanted it?

Damn! He'd really blown it. With all his training and experience in the field of relationships, how could he have disregarded all the rules and let Megan get so close, so involved... And to think he'd been looking forward to her getting more involved, looking forward to all the time he'd have with her during obedience training for the dogs.

Amber! The pup was still at Megan's. Becca would want to go over to Megan's before breakfast and collect the dog as she had every morning since that first night. He couldn't put her through the agony of seeing Megan.

Megan wasn't the only person responsible for this debacle, he knew as he walked across their yards. It was time he admitted his own part in this. He'd made the first overtures and most of the ones after that. He'd pursued her.

But then he'd thought they were building something lasting. What a joke. If there was one thing he'd learned from his years as a psychiatrist, trust was the cornerstone of anything lasting. Megan didn't trust him. On her porch he breathed deeply to steady himself to deal with her one last time. It had to be that way.

Hearing the doorbell, Megan hurriedly swiped at her wet cheeks. Sam had come for Amber, she was sure. She'd already put the dog's leash on her, intending to take the pup back if Sam hadn't thought about it. They both knew it would be better for Becca not to see so much of Megan.

Grabbing up the pup, she sniffed back some more tears, then opened the door.

"I came for..." Sam began, then noted the dog in her arms. "You thought about..."

Megan swallowed around the constriction in her throat. The ice in his eyes was gone, but there was no warmth. Only pain and determination.

"I didn't want Becca to have to come over in the morning," he said, taking the dog. "Under the circumstances... Well, what I should say first is that I know you're not the only one to blame for all this..."

Megan should have expected this from him. Should have known that even now he would be fair. "Thank you, Sam."

He nodded once. "This isn't just between you and me, though. I have to consider Becca. So under the circumstances, I think it's best we don't see each other again."

"Yes," was all she could manage.

She'd thought that Alex had broken her heart, but that pain was nothing compared to the heartrending agony of watching Sam turn his back and walk away.

The quiet and loneliness of the house surrounded Megan as she came home from work Monday. She went outside to find Dusty, but even his puppy-dog antics couldn't dispel the soul-deep emptiness. She was sure nothing ever would.

How could she have fallen so foolishly and deeply in love? Despite all her efforts, she'd ended up where she'd tried too hard not to be—hurt and lonely. Worse yet was the knowledge that she wasn't the only one hurting.

"Dusty," she scolded, catching sight of his latest excavation attempts in her garden. "What is it with you and digging?"

She sat on the bottom deck step and let Dusty climb onto her lap, turning her cheek to receive his doggie kisses. Usually he made her laugh, but tonight all she could think about was spending the rest of her life without Sam.

She put Dusty down and went to water her roses. The ones she'd picked out with Sam's gift certificate. The ones she'd planted Saturday, just before he'd taken her out to dinner.

The night had been magical and romantic. Dancing with Sam ... When she closed her eyes, she could still hear the music, feel the warmth of his body, feel the ache of desire that had filled her then. Had he kissed her good night as she'd wanted him to, had he asked to stay with her, she would have let him. Would have given herself to him gladly and without reservations. Would have ...

Dusty's excited barking broke through her thoughts. She opened her eyes to find Becca standing on the other side of the fence, watching her. Megan could only stare back. How she wanted to take back all she'd done, all the hurt she'd caused the child. Becca, the true innocent, caught in the fallout Megan and Sam had created.

The accusation and pain in Becca's eyes was plain. "My dad says that when you're mad at somebody, you should talk to them about it," she said.

Megan had thought nothing could make her hurt more than she already did, but she'd been wrong. Fate gave the knife in her heart another twist.

"Okay," she said, wishing she could run inside and hide from the recrimination in the five-year-old eyes that glared at her.

She sat on one of the deck chairs and waited for Becca to make the first move. The girl climbed into the chair across from Megan's and studied her shoes for a long moment. Becca was trying very hard not to cry, Megan noticed. The knife plunged deeper into her heart.

"Why don't you want to be our mommy?" Becca finally asked.

Nothing in Megan's life had prepared her for this moment when a small girl would face her and demand to know why Megan was rejecting her.

"Becca..." How could she begin to explain the grown-up world to this small child? "What did your uncle...your daddy tell you?"

"That you had a baby once, before you moved here, and that he died and now you can't have any more babies."

"That's right." Megan sighed, wishing she could find the words to ease the girl's sadness. But nothing she could say would matter. As Sam had pointed out, this was one of those situations where there simply were no words of comfort. "What else did he say?"

"That your baby's daddy left you and now you don't want to get married again. Ever." Becca frowned up at her. "But whenever we went places, you were always laughing and smiling and stuff. Weren't you happy?"

Happier than she'd ever been or would be again, Megan knew. "Yes, I was happy being with you guys."

"I thought you loved us."

How did that old song go: You always hurt the ones you love. Hard as she'd tried not to, she'd loved and hurt the people most important to her.

"I do love you," she said, choosing her words carefully. "As a very special friend. I was very sad when I moved into this house and you loaned me your crayons and paper to help me get over that sadness. I love you because you're such a special person in my life."

Becca's small shoulders rose and fell with her heavy sigh. "I wanted us to keep on being friends. So Dusty and Amber could play and so you could teach me how to draw and paint and make up rhymes. Daddy's not very good with the hard ones."

It was Megan's turn to sigh. Seeing Becca even once in a while would bring back the hurt, make her think of all she'd had and lost, of all that couldn't be. But Becca's needs were the priority. Would a clean break be better for the child, or would it be less painful if Megan gradually eased herself out of the girl's life?

"I have an idea. You can talk it over with Sam, uh, your daddy and see what he says. Maybe I could give you drawing and rhyming lessons every now and then, and Amber can play with Dusty sometimes, too."

"I don't think he'll like that idea. He said we're going to move to a new house so I can make new friends."

The knife dug deeper still. Never to be able to see him again, even from a distance. To know that he was forever beyond her reach. She understood his reasoning, but to think that he never wanted to see her again, that he couldn't bear being as close as next door to her.

"Becca," they heard Sam call from the front porch of his house.

The little girl stood. For a moment Megan thought Becca might hug her. She needed that. Needed any sign, even if it was no more than a tiny smile, that Becca had understood and forgiven her, that the girl would be all right. But Sam called out again, and Becca hurried down the deck steps and out the gate, consigning Megan to an eternity in her own personal hell.

Brian was down for the night, Sam had helped Becca practice her handwriting, then sent her to get into her pajamas. Once she'd brushed her teeth, she came to Sam, ready to be tucked in. She had Megan's book in her hands.

Sam hated the sight of it, and yet it still had the power to draw him at the same time. He knew the singsong phrases by heart, but tonight the rhymes stuck in his throat. Each one held a memory of her, of how easily and naturally she'd fit into his family. He could still recall in vivid detail how he'd felt to come home and find her giving Brian his bedtime bottle, to watch Becca hug her around the waist and announce how much she loved Megan. How it had felt to hold her close.

He'd never thought it possible to feel this alone an empty. As if you'd been hollowed out and nothing woul ever fill your soul again. He wished someone would tell hir just how the hell he would get through the days withou Megan.

And the nights. Last night he'd lain awake, wanting he with every bit of life in his body. Not even the thought tha her lack of trust in him would soon destroy anything the might have had could quell his longing for her. When he' finally managed to doze off, his sleep was fitful and fille with images of her.

At work his secretary had commented on his frequer mental lapses. His partners had also remarked on his in ability to concentrate. To them all he'd blamed the prob lem on a sleepless night due to Brian's teething, just to ge them off his back.

He couldn't tell them the real reason. He simply couldn say the words aloud—that in a few short weeks he'd foun and lost the love of his life. They would be sympathetic, bu they would also try to convince him someone else would on day come along. He'd used that same reasoning with man of his patients. Again Fate stepped in to show him how pa an answer that was. No one but Megan would fill the voi in his life.

Out of the corner of her eye, Megan saw her three friend and co-workers watch her from her office doorway. Sh tried to ignore them as she deleted all the entries she'd mac on the computer worksheet. Somehow she'd entered th data from Marx Dry Cleaners onto the Davidson Constru tion account.

The way she was going it would take all day tomorrow, and maybe half of the next day, to straighten out the two accounts. On top of that, she'd made dozens of transposition errors when she'd copied down the numbers from the Boone Dance Studio's records, and she would have to make another trip out there to figure out which account totals were right and which were wrong.

It had been two weeks and five days since that devastating Sunday she'd last seen Sam. Time was supposed to make things easier, but things were only getting worse.

One of the three in the doorway—Kelly, Liz or Julie—cleared her throat loudly. Megan continued to hit the computer's Delete key.

"You'd think the IRS wanted to audit all her accounts, the way she's been going at it lately," Kelly said.

The truth was it was taking Megan three times longer to do her work. The pain kept getting in the way. And the memories—instead of dulling, they were more and more alive. Often she felt as if she could reach out and touch Sam. Actually feel the warmth in his smile. The love in the way he looked at her.

"No," Julie quipped. "I think she's embezzled and is furiously trying to cover her tracks."

"What I think is that this work can wait." Liz came up behind Megan, grabbed the back of her chair and wheeled her far away from the computer. "Kelly, help me hold her here. Julie, do a Save and shut off the machine."

"Come on," Megan protested weakly. She was precariously close to tears. Crying was all she seemed to do. That and making mistakes. She'd gotten very good at that.

"We're doing this for your own good," Liz informed her.

"Something smells funny," Becca announced, walking into the kitchen.

Dinner, Sam realized a split second before the smoke alarm went off. He turned off the burner, pulled the smoking saucepan off the stove, stuck the pan in the sink, then turned on the water and let it run while he pulled the battery out of the screaming alarm.

The ensuing silence lasted only a second before Brian started crying. Emmaline hadn't been able to get the fussy baby down for a nap until just before Sam got home from the office. Now the damn smoke alarm had startled the boy out of sleep. He changed Brian's diaper, then set him on the kitchen floor while he ordered pizza.

Then he went to work on washing the main course for dinner down the drain. Emmaline had left it for him to reheat and he couldn't even manage that much. But that was par for the course lately. Since he'd sent Megan out of his life, nothing had gone right.

Brian started crying. Becca dropped the plastic pitcher of Kool-Aid on the floor in front of the fridge and just stood there in a big green puddle. The dog began barking. The doorbell rang. In that order. Sam stared, paralyzed, at the chaos in the kitchen alone. Then the doorbell rang again. He was sorely tempted to ignore the damn thing. It was too soon for the pizza and he wasn't expecting anyone.

Joannie. He'd completely forgotten. He rushed to the door to find her there with a couple in their mid-thirties. Sam groaned inwardly. Joannie was here to show the house. He didn't know how he could have forgotten, but he was doing a lot of that these days.

He grabbed up the yipping pup and opened the door to let Joannie and the prospective buyers inside. He turned to see Becca walking into the living room. Her white socks were now green and she left little green puddles wherever she stepped on the beige carpet.

The husband and wife eyed each other, then him and finally Joannie.

"It's been one of those evenings," Sam said by way of explanation. Every day had become one of those days. And the nights were worse—horrors of loneliness and longing and dreams that would never be fulfilled. "Just go ahead and show them around," he told Joannie. "Don't mind us."

He handed the dog to Becca, telling her to take the animal outside, then take off her soaked socks and put them in the laundry room. Then he went to the kitchen and discovered why Brian had quit crying. He'd found the pool of Kool-Aid and was happily sitting in the middle of it, splashing and laughing.

"This is the…" Standing in the doorway, Joannie stopped in midsentence.

Sam turned to see her and the couple behind her staring at Brian. The wife sniffed at the smoky air.

"I cremated dinner and haven't had a chance to bury the ashes yet," Sam said with a tight smile.

"We'll come back," Joannie said tactfully.

Sighing, Sam grabbed the roll of paper towels and started soaking up the deepest parts of Brian's wading pool. The boy wasn't happy with Sam's efforts, though, and made his displeasure known with a loud wail.

"I'm sorry I dropped the pitcher," Becca said, her feet bare as she came into the kitchen, Amber in tow.

The dog sniffed the floor around Brian and began lapping up the Kool-Aid remains. The only useful thing the dog had done to date, Sam thought, tossing the pile of wet paper towels into the trash.

"I'm still thirsty," Becca told him.

Of course she was. He'd just half completed one task. Heaven forbid he should actually get things under control. He poured her a cup of apple juice, then picked up Brian.

As he carried the boy back to his changing table, Sam realized the kid was very warm. Put two and two together—a new tooth coming in, the day-long fussy spell, and now a fever....

Sam groaned to himself again. He just wasn't cut out to handle parenthood alone. But the woman he wanted by his side didn't trust him.

Chapter Twelve

"Three bites," Julie announced as Megan pushed back her plate. "You two owe me a buck apiece. Pay up."

Megan sighed as the other two fished out dollar bills to cover the bet they all must have made before they'd come to drag her out to dinner.

"That long-suffering sigh was one of moping," Kelly stated.

"Mmm," Julie said. "Last month she was mooning. This month she's moping."

"Man trouble," the three said in unison.

"Wanna talk about it?" Liz asked, laying her hand on Megan's.

Megan shook her head. It was still much too painful to discuss, even with Liz.

"Well, the best thing to do," Julie said, "is go out and meet someone new."

"Someone gorgeous to make you forget this other guy," Kelly added.

Someone new. No way did Megan want to risk this kind of heartache again, no matter how gorgeous the package. Besides, no one would ever measure up to Sam Armstrong. No one could be as thoughtful, as compassionate, as generous and loving. No other man's laughter could fill her with happiness. No other man's eyes could shine at her with such tenderness and deep desire. No other man's smile could hold such love.

After dinner Megan wanted to go home, to be alone with her memories and sorrow, but she was outnumbered. And with her car back at the office, she had little say in the matter. The others decided she was going to the movies with them.

In the darkened theater, she remembered the night she'd gone to the movies with Sam. Sitting next to him. Holding his hand. Each time she thought of him, she thought of the For Sale sign in his front yard. One day soon he would be gone from her life. Really gone—physically as well as emotionally.

Somehow she got through the movie, the ride back to the office to pick up her car and the drive home. Dusty was yipping at the back door. When she let him in, he went directly to his bowls, drank noisily, then turned his attention to his food. As Megan dropped her purse and keys on the kitchen countertop, she realized she'd forgotten to check the mailbox before driving into the garage. She was tempted to let it go until tomorrow, but she'd let too many things slide lately.

Halfway across her lawn, she heard Sam's front door open. Brian was screaming, a full-fledged, frightening scream. Megan's breath caught. Something was seriously wrong.

It's not your place to be concerned anymore, she admonished herself, but hearing the intensity of Brian's cries, she couldn't shut off her worry.

"Why do we have to go to the hospital?" Becca asked plaintively, her voice raised over her brother's wailing.

"Because the doctor's there," Sam snapped, his frustration clear.

Juggling Brian, he unlocked the van in the driveway. When the dome light came on, Megan could see that with every scream, Brian twisted and squirmed, resisting Sam's efforts with all his strength. Sam couldn't get the boy's small body into the car seat because Brian thrashed so furiously.

Megan didn't hesitate. She raced over to the van. "Get in and buckle up, honey," she told Becca, who stood there in her sneakers and pajamas, watching the scene with wide, frightened eyes. "Sam." Megan had to shout to be heard over Brian.

Sam whirled to face her. What was she doing here, just when he most needed someone? Needed her. No, his mind protested with all its might. He couldn't let her close again. Not even for a few minutes.

"Sam, I know how you feel," she said. "But you need another pair of hands and mine are the only ones available."

It nearly killed Megan to see the first warmth in his eyes give way to the cold and the pain. He was shutting her out. But there was no time to think about her own heartache while Brian was clearly suffering.

"Okay," Sam finally said. "Can you drive? I can't get him to stay in the car seat and I doubt you're strong enough to hold him."

Megan nodded. She ran home to get her purse and house keys, then raced back to the van. Sam gave her directions to the hospital while he struggled to hold onto Brian and keep him from injuring himself. Each of the boy's screams tore at Megan's heart.

"What do you think it is?" she asked Sam as they pulled up to the hospital and sprinted to the ER entrance.

"Another ear infection. I hope."

One of the ER nurses came out as soon as they were inside. "Dr. Rossiter said to get you in right away," she said as she whisked Sam and Brian through the exam area's doors.

With the whoosh of the automatic doors, he and the baby were gone. Megan took her first deep breath since hearing Brian's cries of pain. She led Becca to the waiting room. Becca climbed into one of the chairs, looking tiny and frightened.

"The doctors will make Brian better," Megan told her. "He'll be fine," she added when Becca didn't respond. "Probably it's just that his ear hurts really bad."

Becca remained silent, her expression afraid. Megan longed to be able to take the girl on her lap and comfort her, but it wasn't fair for Megan to pull and tug on Becca's emotions. Megan found a couple of children's books and brought them over to Becca. She took the books, but didn't look at them.

"Becca," Megan said softly as Brian's crying carried out from the exam room. "Talk to me, honey. It's going to be all right."

Becca looked up, her eyes filling with tears. "My mommy and daddy went to the hospital."

Hearing the naked pain and fear in the girl's voice, Megan pulled Becca on her lap and held her close. Right or wrong, she needed comfort and Megan couldn't deny her.

"Your brother will be okay," she said in a crooning manner.

"Th-that's what Uncle, I mean Daddy said about my mommy and my real daddy."

Megan held her tightly, rocking her as her tiny shoulders shook with her sobs.

"Honey, that was different," Megan explained. "They were in a car accident. Brian only has an earache."

Becca looked up at her. "But why does he cry so hard?"

"Earaches can be very painful and he's just a baby. All he knows to do when he hurts is cry."

"Oh." She wiped her nose on a tissue Megan handed her. "I still wish you could be my mommy. I would be real good," she rushed to add before Megan could protest.

Megan thought her heart would break at the earnest plea. There was nothing she wanted more than to say yes. But she couldn't. How to make the child understand that you couldn't always have what you wanted, even if you wanted it more than life itself?

What could she have done differently? She thought of how lonely she was, of how empty the rest of her days would be. As Becca lay her head on Megan's breast while they waited for the doctor to treat Brian, Megan silently cursed the unfairness of it all.

Carrying a whimpering Brian, Sam walked into the waiting room an hour later to find Megan holding a tearful Becca. His first thought was that she—Megan—was exactly who they all needed to make them whole.

Then he decided that if he felt anything, it should be anger. He should be absolutely furious with Megan. He'd had difficulty enough trying to explain to Becca why Megan couldn't be there. Now he would have to start all over again.

"Is he all right?" she asked, looking up at him with eyes full of concern.

"Another ear infection—both ears this time," he said, noting the relief in her gaze. "Andy gave him a shot and some stronger eardrops for the pain. He's going to set up an appointment with an ENT for Monday morning to see if we can't figure out why Brian's getting so many of them."

"Becca was really worried," she told him.

He sat in the seat beside them, hitched Brian up higher on his shoulder and held out his free arm for his daughter. She scrambled off Megan's lap and into his embrace. Over the top of Becca's head he gazed at Megan. His breath caught at the longing he saw there as she watched him hug his children. Again he was hit by how much love she had.

And by how much he loved her. His need for her had only grown during their separation. Now, after these very precious moments with her helping him deal with another crisis, he didn't know how he could go back to living without her. Or how he could live with himself, remembering that wistful look in her eyes.

Reviving himself after his battle with the ER staff, Brian began to fuss, then cry. He raised his head and spotted Megan. As he had that first day on her deck, and so many times since, he reached for her.

She looked to Sam for permission and Sam realized he hated seeing that hesitation. Hated knowing she felt she couldn't reach out and take what she so obviously wanted and needed with every ounce of breath in her body. He understood. She didn't want to intrude or cause them any more pain, but he hated it just the same.

The moment he placed his son in her arms, the boy nestled against her breasts. With his thumb in his mouth, he reached to pat her cheek with his free hand.

"See," Becca stated. "Brian still likes Megan best."

Megan tried to smile, but couldn't manage it. This would be the last time. The last time she would hold this baby and see him look up at her with such loving eyes. The last time she would comfort Becca while the girl sat on her lap. The last time she would see Sam, have him close enough that she could inhale the all-male scent of him. Hear the sound of his voice. Have him gaze at her with tenderness and fiery passion.

"Can you manage him?" he asked, a tremble in his voice.

She nodded, not trusting her own voice.

Once they were outside, he settled Becca next to her in the van's middle seat, pulling the safety belt securely around her. His handsome face would fill her dreams for a long time to come, Megan knew. She could see the stubble of his beard and wished that just once she could feel the rough texture of it against her skin as he made love to her.

As he drove, she studied his strong profile, committing each line to memory—the firm jut of his chin, the angle of his well-shaped nose, even the curves of his perfect ears. Details to keep him alive in her thoughts.

Too soon he was pulling the van into his driveway. As he helped Becca out, Megan had a moment to prepare herself to let Brian go. But not even a lifetime would be long enough to ready herself to give him up. With a determined breath, she shifted the weight in her arms, but when Sam tried to take him, Brian batted at his hands and cried.

Sam stopped wrestling with the boy and watched him settle back into Megan's arms. The kid knew what he wanted and he knew what Megan was giving him—comfort, caring, love. Yeah, the boy knew what he wanted and he knew how to fight to keep it.

"Would you bring him inside?" Sam asked, not completely sure why he didn't want to let her go.

Her eyes lit with happiness, then the brightness dimmed. He sensed she was thinking about the time when she would leave. Did she have any idea how lonely he would be without her?

Sam guided Megan out of the van, his hands strong and warm on her elbow and her back. He stayed close to her, touching the small of her back, his shoulder brushing hers as they walked up the porch steps and into the house.

Her heart already breaking, she headed down the hall to Brian's room. The baby didn't want to be put in his bed, though. He cried and reached for her, his eyes pleading.

"Maybe if you gave him his bottle," Sam suggested from behind her.

She nodded, then settled in the rocking chair, grateful for the excuse to prolong her leaving and puzzled at Sam's willingness to let her stay.

Becca walked in a short while later with a bottle of formula. "Daddy said I could kiss you good night," she said.

Megan didn't understand his actions, but she would gladly take the kiss of love and affection from this golden-haired pixie. Brian held his bottle, freeing Megan to hug Becca. Then Megan glanced up to find Sam watching the scene, his expression unreadable. He must know he was only making her leaving harder on everyone, but he didn't rush Becca. Only when she was ready to say good night did he step away from the doorway and follow her to her bedroom.

Megan blinked back her tears. If she had only a few brief moments left here with his children and him, she wouldn't waste the time in regret. She savored the sleepy smile Brian gave her, the way his hand closed around her finger, and watched his eyes flutter closed. Long after he'd quit sucking on the bottle, she held him.

She didn't know how long she'd sat there rocking him before she heard Sam in the doorway. She steeled herself to let Sam take Brian, but instead he just stood there, gazing down at her with an earnestness she didn't understand.

"There's something I have to tell you," he said quietly.

Megan bit her lip, waiting for the words that would end all the wonderful things they'd shared.

"I've been pacing the living room for the last half hour," he continued. "Trying to reason myself out of love with you."

Her heart missed a beat. What was he saying? She opened her mouth, but nothing came out. In her arms, Brian slept, peacefully unaware of the hope and apprehension pounding through her.

"I told myself that relationships take time. I've helped dozens of people pick up the pieces when one falls apart." He ran a hand across his square jaw. "I told myself we barely know each other—"

"That I didn't trust you?" she prompted softly.

"Yeah." He knelt beside the rocking chair. "We've only known each other for what, a month? Six weeks, tops. So how the hell can I be in love with you?"

The words she'd never dared dream he would say to her. She looked deep into his sapphire eyes, feeling herself standing at the edge of a cliff, dizzy from the height, knowing she had to take the plunge.

"I don't know," she said in a whisper, "but I do know I love you, too. I tried not to. I really did. I was so afraid..." Her voice cracked. A lone tear trickled down her cheek.

Sam caught the teardrop with the back of his hand, his fingers lingering against the softness of her skin. Suddenly he wanted to touch all of her, to feel her slender body pressed against him, to be inside her, loving her until they were too exhausted to question this love they felt for each other.

They had so much to work out, he knew, but the love and commitment were there. In the living room, knowing she was here rocking Brian to sleep, he'd decided he had to try to reach her. He couldn't live without her. Couldn't they find a way to make it work?

He started to draw her to him only to be reminded she still held Brian. The boy hardly stirred as Sam lifted him from Megan's arms and laid him in the crib. Sam walked back to her and tugged her out of the rocker and into his embrace. She clung to him with a ferocity that told him how very much she loved him and how very frightened she was by the strength of these feelings.

They scared the hell out of him. This need that wouldn't be controlled or denied. This tenderness that stole over him at unsuspecting moments. This passion that only grew stronger each time he was near her.

He captured her mouth and drank greedily of her sweetness, knowing there would be no more holding back. Her breasts rose and fell with each ragged breath she took.

Megan felt his fire engulf her. Waves of need tore through her. She ached, throbbed with desire. Sam loved her, wanted her with a desperation as strong as what she felt for him. But would that be enough? She couldn't lose him a second time. She couldn't. Couldn't.

He pulled away to look down at her, and Megan realized she was crying. He dried her tears, kissed her cheeks. Then he took her hand and led her to his bedroom. In the doorway, he bent to pick her up and carry her to the bed. His bed. Her breath caught as he lay beside her and gathered her close.

"I love you," he told her.

"Oh, Sam, I love you." She didn't mean to cry, but she couldn't seem to stop.

"Happy tears?" he asked.

She nodded. "And I... I couldn't bear it if..."

"If it all fell apart?" he asked, saying the words she couldn't. When she nodded, he kissed her forehead. "I couldn't stand it, either. So then we're agreed that staying together is our first priority."

Yes. Oh, yes, her heart shouted, but there was still one thing it couldn't drown out. "Children," she said, knowing they had to deal with this issue. "You told Becca you wanted more children."

"Marry me and we'll have two—Becca and Brian. And if they aren't enough of a handful, there are a lot of children in need of the love you and I could give them."

Megan felt sure her heart would explode with happiness, but there was still this tiny bit of her mind that urged caution. "Just like that you'll give up the possibility of having children of your own?"

"Not just like that. I wrestled with that one for a while." He chuckled wryly. "You don't realize how many times I imagined you carrying my child."

"But that can't be."

"So I asked myself exactly how important that was. Each time I weigh all the choices, I choose you."

"Even though you think I don't trust you?" She didn't want to ask, but she had to.

"Well, I was going to get around to that pretty soon. I worked out this theory that maybe at first it was too hard for you to share everything with a stranger. Then later—call it wishful thinking on my part, but I hoped it was because you were afraid I would pull back."

Megan did what she'd wanted to do earlier. She stroked his cheek, glorying in the roughness of his beard. "How do you read me so well?"

He turned his head and kissed her palm. "I got lucky this time." He kissed the pulse beat at her wrist. "In the future, though, no more secrets. I need you to share everything with me, Megan."

Everything. Yes, that's the way she wanted it to be, too. "What about Christmas and birthday presents?" she teased.

His laughter rumbled in his chest. "I'll just have to devise ways to get you to spill your guts. Creative ways."

Before she could take a breath, she found herself flat on her back and staring up at him. At the love in his smile. Then warmth turned to heat and all she could think about was the wonder of his kiss, the joy of his hands sliding under her blouse to caress her skin.

"Daddy," a little voice said from the doorway. "I couldn't sle— Megan?"

Megan floated back to earth and found herself exactly where she belonged. She laughed softly at the frustration she saw in Sam's eyes.

"Is Megan going to sleep here?" Becca asked, obviously bewildered at seeing Megan in Sam's bed.

"Come here, squirt." Sam patted the bed on the other side of Megan.

"I couldn't go back to sleep," she said, scrambling up.

"Well, then, as long as you're awake, do you still want Megan to be your mom?"

Becca's eyes widened with sheer happiness, then narrowed in confusion. "Really be my mom? Like Mommy was? And she'll live here with us and everything?"

Sam nodded. "I was about to ask her to marry me."

Becca bounced excitedly on the bed. "Marry all of us! Say yes, Megan. Say yes."

"Yes." Megan laughed. "I'll marry all of you."

Becca threw her arms around Megan's neck. "Yea! I can't wait to tell Francie. I'm going to have a daddy *and* a mommy again. And now Megan won't have to buy furniture."

Sam and Megan looked at each other and laughed. "She's got it all worked out." Sam shook his head in wonder.

"Can I tell Francie?" she persisted.

"In the morning," Sam told her. "And only if you're in bed and sound asleep in five minutes flat."

She hurriedly jumped off the bed. At the door she stopped. "Is Megan going to be here when I wake up?"

"Yes, she will," Sam replied.

"Don't I have a say in this?" Megan asked once they were alone.

Sam leaned over her, a lecherous gleam in his eyes. "You can say anything you want, as long as you say it while I'm making love to you."

But no sooner did he get the words out than Brian started to cry again. With a growl, Sam watched Megan get up to get the poor kid. "Not exactly the way I planned to celebrate," he said, following her into Brian's room.

Megan smiled at him. "Is Emmaline coming tomorrow?"

He nodded, then brightened. "Are you thinking what I'm thinking?"

"That we could sneak off to my place—"

"Not far away enough. But I know this classy hotel."

As he went for the telephone to make the reservations, Megan settled in the rocking chair. Brian would be her son. Becca would be her daughter. They would be her family. And through all the joys and upsets and worries, Sam would be by her side.

*   *   *   *   *

Get Ready to be Swept Away by
Silhouette's Spring Collection

Abduction
Seduction

These passion-filled stories explore both the dangerous
desires of men and the seductive powers of women.
Written by three of our most celebrated authors, they are
sure to capture your hearts.

Diana Palmer
Brings us a spin-off of her Long, Tall Texans series

Joan Johnston
Crafts a beguiling Western romance

Rebecca Brandewyne
New York Times bestselling author
makes a smashing contemporary debut

Available in March at your favorite retail outlet.

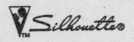

MILLION DOLLAR SWEEPSTAKES (III)

No purchase necessary. To enter, follow the directions published. Method of entry may vary. For eligibility, entries must be received no later than March 31, 1996. No liability is assumed for printing errors, lost, late or misdirected entries. Odds of winning are determined by the number of eligible entries distributed and received. Prizewinners will be determined no later than June 30, 1996.

Sweepstakes open to residents of the U.S. (except Puerto Rico), Canada, Europe and Taiwan who are 18 years of age or older. All applicable laws and regulations apply. Sweepstakes offer void wherever prohibited by law. Values of all prizes are in U.S. currency. This sweepstakes is presented by Torstar Corp., its subsidiaries and affiliates, in conjunction with book, merchandise and/or product offerings. For a copy of the Official Rules send a self-addressed, stamped envelope (WA residents need not affix return postage) to: MILLION DOLLAR SWEEPSTAKES (III) Rules, P.O. Box 4573, Blair, NE 68009, USA.

EXTRA BONUS PRIZE DRAWING

No purchase necessary. The Extra Bonus Prize will be awarded in a random drawing to be conducted no later than 5/30/96 from among all entries received. To qualify, entries must be received by 3/31/96 and comply with published directions. Drawing open to residents of the U.S. (except Puerto Rico), Canada, Europe and Taiwan who are 18 years of age or older. All applicable laws and regulations apply; offer void wherever prohibited by law. Odds of winning are dependent upon number of eligible entries received. Prize is valued in U.S. currency. The offer is presented by Torstar Corp., its subsidiaries and affiliates in conjunction with book, merchandise and/or product offering. For a copy of the Official Rules governing this sweepstakes, send a self-addressed, stamped envelope (WA residents need not affix return postage) to: Extra Bonus Prize Drawing Rules, P.O. Box 4590, Blair, NE 68009, USA.

SWP-S295

The Loop ™

Is the future what it's cracked up to be?

This February, find out if Emily's marriage
can be saved in

GETTING OUT: EMILY
by ArLynn Presser

When Emily said "I do," she had vowed to love Marsh
forever. And she still loved him, but marriage wasn't
as easy as her parents made it look! Getting married
so young had been hard enough, but now that she
was going back to school, things were getting even
worse. She wanted to meet new people and try
different things, but all Marsh wanted to do was
cocoon! Suddenly the decisions that had seemed so
right just a few years ago seemed totally wrong.

The ups and downs of life as you know it continue with

GETTING AWAY WITH IT: JOJO
by Liz Ireland (March)

GETTING A CLUE: TAMMY
by Wendy Mass (April)

Get smart. Get into "The Loop!"

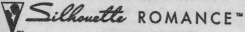

SILHOUETTE... Where Passion Lives

Don't miss these Silhouette favorites by some of our most distinguished authors! And now you can receive a discount by ordering two or more titles!

SD#05786	QUICKSAND by Jennifer Greene	$2.89	☐
SD#05795	DEREK by Leslie Guccione	$2.99	☐
SD#05818	NOT JUST ANOTHER PERFECT WIFE		
	by Robin Elliott	$2.99	☐
IM#07505	HELL ON WHEELS by Naomi Horton	$3.50	☐
IM#07514	FIRE ON THE MOUNTAIN		
	by Marion Smith Collins	$3.50	☐
IM#07559	KEEPER by Patricia Gardner Evans	$3.50	☐
SSE#09879	LOVING AND GIVING by Gina Ferris	$3.50	☐
SSE#09892	BABY IN THE MIDDLE	$3.50 U.S.	☐
	by Marie Ferrarella	$3.99 CAN.	
SSE#09902	SEDUCED BY INNOCENCE	$3.50 U.S.	☐
	by Lucy Gordon	$3.99 CAN.	
SR#08952	INSTANT FATHER by Lucy Gordon	$2.75	☐
SR#08984	AUNT CONNIE'S WEDDING		
	by Marie Ferrarella	$2.75	☐
SR#08990	JILTED by Joleen Daniels	$2.75	☐

(limited quantities available on certain titles)

AMOUNT	$_____
DEDUCT: 10% DISCOUNT FOR 2+ BOOKS	$_____
POSTAGE & HANDLING	$_____
($1.00 for one book, 50¢ for each additional)	
APPLICABLE TAXES*	$_____
TOTAL PAYABLE	$_____
(check or money order—please do not send cash)	

To order, complete this form and send it, along with a check or money order for the total above, payable to Silhouette Books, to: **In the U.S.:** 3010 Walden Avenue, P.O. Box 9077, Buffalo, NY 14269-9077; **In Canada:** P.O. Box 636, Fort Erie, Ontario, L2A 5X3.

Name:_____

Address:_____City:_____

State/Prov.:_____ Zip/Postal Code:_____

*New York residents remit applicable sales taxes.
 Canadian residents remit applicable GST and provincial taxes.

SBACK-DF

Silhouette®
™